I0761278

SACRED LIGHT

A selection of titles from Kathryn Lasky

The Georgia O'Keeffe Mysteries

LIGHT ON BONE
MORTAL RADIANCE *
A SLANT OF LIGHT *

The Guardians of Ga'Hoole Series

THE HATCHLING
THE OUTCAST
THE FIRST COLLIER
THE COMING OF HOOLE
EXILE
THE WAR OF THE EMBER
THE RISE OF A LEGEND

The Secret of Glendunny Series

THE SECRET OF GLENDUNNY: THE HAUNTING
THE SEARCHERS

The Tangled in Time Series

THE PORTAL
THE BURNING QUEEN

The Bears of the Ice Series

THE QUEST OF THE CUBS
DEN OF FOREVER FROST
THE KEEPERS OF THE KEYS

Novels

THE NIGHT JOURNEY
NIGHT WITCHES
FACELESS
GLASS

* *available from Severn House*

Visit www.kathrynlasky.com for a full list of titles

SACRED LIGHT

Kathryn Lasky

First world edition published in Great Britain and the USA in 2026
by Severn House, an imprint of Canongate Books Ltd,
14 High Street, Edinburgh EH1 1TE.

severnhouse.com

Cover and jacket design by Nick May at bluegecko22.com

British Library Cataloguing-in-Publication Data
A CIP catalogue record for this title is available from the British Library.

ISBN-13: 978-1-4483-1656-4 (cased)
ISBN-13: 978-1-4483-1886-5 (paper)
ISBN-13: 978-1-4483-1655-7 (e-book)

All Severn House titles are printed on acid-free paper.

Typeset by Palimpsest Book Production Ltd., Falkirk, Stirlingshire, Scotland.
Printed and bound in Great Britain by TJ Books, Padstow, Cornwall.

The manufacturer's authorised representative in the EU for product safety is Authorised Rep Compliance Ltd, 71 Lower Baggot Street, Dublin D02 P593 Ireland (arccompliance.com)

Praise for the Georgia O'Keeffe Mysteries

"Readers will be enchanted by the descriptions of the Southwest landscape seen through Georgia's artistic eye. Fans of historical mysteries that feature real-life people will enjoy this series"
Booklist

"The Land of Enchantment is the perfect backdrop for a murder investigation among historic characters both artistic and evil"
Kirkus Reviews

"The intricately plotted mystery puts a new spin on several historical figures . . . Lasky provides vivid descriptions through O'Keeffe's eyes that bring the setting and timeframe to life"
Library Journal Starred Review

"Step aside Miss Marple, Eugenia Potter, and Kinsey Millhone—Georgia O'Keeffe is the new sleuth in town!"
Katherine Hall Page, author of the award-winning Faith Fairchild series

"Kathryn Lasky draws Georgia O'Keeffe's New Mexico with her own skillful hand . . . I couldn't put it down"
Gregory Maguire, author of *Wicked*

"O'Keeffe's righteous vision does not flinch from the truth, and we follow her gaze in fascination through this masterfully woven story"
Joseph Finder, *New York Times* bestselling author of *Judgment* and *House on Fire*

About the author

Kathryn Lasky is the author of over one hundred books for children and young adults, including the Guardians of Ga'Hoole series, which has more than eight million copies in print, and was turned into a major motion picture, *Legend of the Guardians: The Owls of Ga'Hoole*.

Her books have received numerous awards including a Newbery Honor, a Boston Globe-Horn Book Award, and a Washington Post-Children's Book Guild Nonfiction Award. She has twice won the National Jewish Book award. Her work has been translated into nineteen languages worldwide. Her newest series is an adult historical mystery series featuring real-life painter Georgia O'Keeffe, who is considered one of the most significant artists of the twentieth century. Kathryn lives with her husband in Cambridge, MA.

www.kathrynlasky.com

PROLOGUE

There was a bite out of the moon as the old man with his hunched back and walking stick made his way across the desolate, gray landscape. Leading his burro, Pedro, he printed a large shadow against the lighter gray of ancient riverbeds. Then the bands of darker layers of congealed ash and slippery black clay began to rise, lifting into the night, and marching across the sky 'like a mile of elephants', as Miss O'Keeffe often said. She painted with her words as much as with her brush, Juan thought as he regarded the humps of the hills that loomed on the crest.

Had the clouds that night not taken the bite from the moon, making it what his great-grandmother called a Coyote Moon, one could have seen those elephants more clearly. It gave the old man the shivers. The Coyote would be up to mischief on nights like these. For it was on just such a night that Coyote came for the First Woman and shook out her star blanket, making a grand confusion of the stars she had so carefully placed in the sky. But he thought he had seen shadows against the cliffs in the moonlight. Or was it a beam of light from his guide star, Náhookòs Bikò, the North Star?

However, now a mist had rolled across the cliffs. This gave him the shivers. The cliffs were where the Navajo suspended the wrapped bodies of their dead high in the trees to protect them from scavengers. And the swirling mists were said to come when the souls were restless or disturbed. They called such mists the chindi, ghosts. But then again there were footprints here as if leading down from the cliffs. He chuckled to himself. "Chindi don't leave footprints," he murmured.

But now, no more than fifty feet ahead, he saw something that gave him a quiet thrill. He forgot about the swirling chindi in the mists that crept down from the cliffs. The shadowy chindi of restless souls. He suddenly felt blessed as a set—yes, a complete set—of a mule deer buck's antlers rose. They hung like a chandelier in the night. They were beautiful.

"Oh, Miss O'Keeffe," he sighed. "You're going to love these!"

He pulled on the lead line of his burro. "Come along, Pedro. Come along," he urged.

As he tipped his head up to scan the night, he didn't notice another shadow sliding across the land, a figure with an ax lifted high as it sliced through the night. Juan dropped to the ground. Blood poured from his shoulder as he lay bleeding in the ancient riverbed. The clouds dissolved and a constellation reappeared, framed between the branching antlers of the mule deer. *Oh, Señora O'Keeffe*, he thought again, *what a painting these would make! I collect bones for you, and now you will collect mine!*

"Vaya con dios," a voice grunted. And Pedro the donkey collapsed in a pool of blood.

ONE

The Ghost Ranch. Abiquiu, New Mexico. July 1937

"Finally!" Georgia said, sitting up in bed.

"Finally . . . what?" Ryan McCaffrey yawned.

"No clouds."

"So, you can go to the Black Place?"

"Yes, at last. Ansel is jumping out of his skin to get there again. So's the other guy he came with."

"Who's that?" Ryan asked.

"Oh, a fellow—David Mc . . . something or other. Very rich, related to the Rockefellers somehow, and starting a photography center at Princeton. He couldn't believe it when he heard Ansel Adams was coming out. Princeton I guess has acquired some of Ansel's photography."

"So where are you going to camp?"

"Well, there's an archaeology dig going on out there—from Yale. We'll most likely camp near them." She paused. "Not too near, I hope."

"Why's that?"

"You know me."

"Now what do you mean by that?"

"Gets too crowded when I want to paint. I've been yearning to go back to the Black Place for a long time. And I've seen those archaeology digs. They bring a mess of people—a cook, wranglers, volunteers, or maybe big donors who want to try their hand at a little digging."

"Are you trying to tell me you're not social, Georgia?"

"Yeah, possibly. Nevertheless, it's good to be in some proximity just in case there is an emergency of some sort. A couple of years ago, there were some people and one of them had appendicitis. Orville raced into Far Cry on his horse and came back with his truck to transport the fellow."

"How about me? Could I go?"

"You can't. You are the sheriff; your job awaits you. By the way, I got a letter from Joseph today. He seems to be enjoying his time with my sister. Let me read it to you. You'll get a kick out of this."

She reached toward the bedside table and picked up a folded piece of paper.

Dear Toto,

Auntie Claudia is teaching me to play tennis. She says I'm getting better every day. I think I might be able to beat her in another week or so. Auntie Claudia is a very good cook. Almost better than you. It's nice here but almost too pretty. I miss the desert—and you too, and Ryan. I wish Auntie Claudia had more good books to read like you do. I tried one called War and Piece, but I gave up on it.

"'Peace' by the way is spelled 'P-i-e-c-e'," Georgia added and then continued:

But all the names were really long, and used about half the whole alphabet for one single name. Can you beat that? Auntie Claudia said that was how they did it in Russia. I'm glad I don't live in Russia.

Love,
Joseph

"Ha!" Ryan laughed. "Tennis and *War and Peace*. Wow!" He leaned over and tipped Georgia's face up to give her a kiss. "Well, he sounds fairly happy and that's what counts. You're raising a good kid, Georgia."

"I'm not raising him. He was raised by his parents. I just rescued him from St. Ignatius."

"You're raising him too."

"He was good to start with. He just required a course correction, so to speak, after enduring all those years at that school."

"Don't underestimate yourself."

Georgia made a half-grunting noise. Her modesty was offended by what she considered undue praise.

Joseph Reyes was an orphan that Georgia had rescued from an abusive Indian boarding school seven months before. She was in the process of trying to adopt him. In the meantime, she had sent him to spend a few weeks with her sister Claudia, who was a teacher in California. He and Claudia had bonded when she had come to New Mexico for a visit in the spring. They'd hiked together, gone fishing, and rode horses. Of all her sisters, she knew that Claudia and Joseph would bond the best. Hard to imagine Joseph in New York City living with her sister Anita in her fancy Park Avenue apartment, or in Palm Beach at her mansion there. But youngest sister Claudia was a sweet, plain-spoken woman and a fantastic schoolteacher. While she was here, she had taught Joseph more math than he had ever learned in all his years at the dreadful St. Ignatius school. At the end of the four weeks in California, Joseph would be back to start public school in Santa Fe. And Georgia would, hopefully, have some new paintings to send to her husband, Stieglitz, at his gallery for the show he hoped to mount in the fall.

So, this two-week packhorse trip into the Bisti Badlands was perfectly timed. The Badlands was one of her favorite landscapes to paint. She called it the Black Place and it was eternally fascinating. She sometimes called it The Faraway too. And it seemed to Georgia that her intention as an artist was to bring the faraway closer, to pare it down to just a few elements. And then one could begin to see what she saw. To really see, not just look. Seeing was so different from just looking. To see was to find something of oneself possibly in a painting. It was in a sense a kind of visual transubstantiation.

"So, when do you leave for the Black Place?" Ryan asked.

"Crack of dawn tomorrow. We are, or rather Orville is, trailering with the packhorses out to Far Cry, and we'll ride the horses in from there. I'm riding in with Orville, and Ansel. You do know Ansel Adams, right?"

"Never met him, but I sure do admire his photographs. Mattie had a few of his books."

"Well, as I said, he'll be along with this fellow from Princeton. They will follow. And then there is the archaeologist from Yale, Douglas something or other, who has his own car. We're all having dinner tonight together up at the Hacienda."

"Sounds like my kind of crowd—Princeton, Yale."

"Now, Ryan, don't go all snooty."

"How could I get snooty? Think about it, they're here to study me and my ancestors who were out here before the first toe of a pilgrim ever touched Plymouth Rock."

Georgia chuckled.

"What about Orville? He's a wrangler. Will he fit in?" Ryan asked.

"Orville can wrangle anything, from a bunch of snooty guests going for a trail ride to a wild bull. Remember when that two-bit supposed royalty from—where was it? Albania?—came here? He was a prince and he and Orville wound up to be great buddies. He even invited Orville to go sturgeon fishing with him in Albania."

"Are there sturgeon in Albania?"

"You're asking me?" Georgia said. "Speaking of fishing, when are you and Linc going bass fishing?"

"That's weeks away, but it should be great. Okeechobee, here we come!"

"Where is that?"

"Florida. Best largemouth bass fishing in the world—so Linc tells me. Micropterus salmoides, look out!"

"Micro-what?"

"Micropterus salmoides, Latin for largemouth bass. And I didn't even go to Yale."

"I know, you're such a smarty pants."

He walked over and gave her a big hug.

"Going to miss you, darling," he whispered in her ear.

"And me you." She pinched his butt.

"Don't get into trouble when you're away."

"Now why would you say that? I don't get into trouble." As soon as the words were out of her mouth, she remembered the trouble from the last time they were apart.

"Need I remind you, Georgia, that when you were in Taos and I was in San Francisco at that conference, you seem to have had a run-in with both the mafia and Nazis. Double header if there ever was one. That takes real talent!"

"Oh, that." Georgia almost blushed.

"Yes, that! The company you keep, Georgia O'Keeffe."

"You're talking about Bugsy Siegel, I guess. I hardly kept him company. I nearly finished him off with his own Gilly Teen, that snake killing device."

"That's the rattlesnake thing you were telling me about that you snipped off his trigger finger with, right?"

"Self-defense, and somewhere I heard that he got it sewn back on in prison. Probably with taxpayer money." She sniffed.

"You want to demand a refund on your taxes?"

"Don't be silly. Speaking of sewing things, that shirt you're wearing when you came today has a rip in it. I thought you were going to mend it."

"Didn't get to it."

"It's a nice shirt. One of your few spiffy ones."

"I'm not spiffy enough for you every day? This, by the way, is a McCaffrey plaid shirt. Green and black. Clan colors."

"Snazzy! Usually, you're wearing your sheriff's outfit."

"You make it sound like it's a costume. It's a uniform. But OK, I'll mend it."

"If you mend it you could come to dinner with me tonight at the Hacienda; the people should be interesting."

"Professors and the like? East coast intellectuals."

"Not Ansel, and where do you get away with dismissing an entire coast of this country?"

"It's the only shirt I brought, and I promise I'll mend it so we can go out to dinner together when you get back from the Black Place."

"Fair enough." Georgia smiled, then walked over to him and pulled down his pants that he had just put on. "How about one for the road before you go?"

"Georgia, darlin', you're getting very aggressive."

"Who, me?" She looked down and tried to bat her eyes.

"Jean Harlow?" Ryan asked. "Who needs Jean Harlow when I have Georgia O'Keeffe?" They fell into bed again.

TWO

"Well, we have made some very exciting discoveries in the last two weeks."

Professor Douglas Acheson was "swoonable", as Georgia's sister Anita might have said. Movie-star handsome, very similar to Hollywood heart throb Gary Cooper. Blond, strong features, the quintessential American hero.

"Exciting in what way?" Ansel Adams' friend David McAlpin asked.

"You see, since archaeologists first started digging out here, maybe thirty years ago, plus or minus a few years, the earliest pottery found came from Anasazi ruins like Mesa Verde in Colorado or Chaco Canyon. Harvard has been very busy there. Those pots or fragments were dated around 900 AD. But we have found some on our site that predate that. Much older." He inhaled deeply and scanned the others at the table with his deep blue eyes. "There is no absolute way of dating artifacts, although people at Massachusetts Institute of Technology and some folks at the University of Chicago are working on something called radiocarbon dating that looks promising and could yield absolute dating. We can only use comparison right now, or relative dating."

"Which means what?" Ansel asked.

"It means comparing it to something older or younger in the stratigraphy. That is the scientific study of rock layers or strata and their arrangement in space and time. So, we dug down and began to find something quite ancient in the oldest stratification in our site—fragments of an unusual style of Anasazi pottery. It still bore some of the primitive designs but was different stylistically. And most interesting of all, there is some evidence that the designs were carved by a fragment of a mastodon's tooth." He paused as if to let that fact sink in. "Mastodons lived in the late Holocene period. That's thousands of years ago."

There were gasps around the table.

"Who knew mastodons were such artists!" Georgia said. The people around the table appeared startled until they realized she was joking and burst out laughing.

"But I don't quite understand," Georgia said.

"What don't you understand, Miss O'Keeffe?" Acheson paused for just a second. "By the way, one of our most important sponsors for this dig owns I think two of your paintings."

Georgia gave a curt smile. She never knew what to say in these situations.

"I guess I am saying that the mastodon tooth was used as a tool for the artist, right?"

"Yes."

"So, the artist could have been walking about and just happened on this tooth, and thought, 'Ah ha, I could use this to carve a design in some rock, or pottery or whatever.' In other words, an accident of proximity."

"Interesting supposition, but one must also consider the context. It was found in a very ancient strata and the tooth itself was incised with a very ancient symbol, a sort of proto, if I may, rainbow that became ubiquitous and more refined a millennium later."

It seemed to Georgia that the professor was conflating two things—the age of the design carved in the pottery and the age of the tool. That they were found close to each other was, in her mind, pure accident. The land out here was volatile—flash flood, earthquakes, constant erosion. The fact that an ancient design and an ancient tooth could be found close to each other, in the same strata, did not seem in any way extraordinary to her.

"Hmm," Georgia responded. "I guess we can conclude that the artist was lucky to survive and not have been stampeded or crushed by the mastodon."

"I'm not saying, Miss O'Keeffe, that the artist brought the mastodon down. It must have already been dead. But the context is most interesting."

Georgia nodded. "I suppose so." She paused for several

seconds. "But that doesn't mean," Georgia said, "that the mastodon and the humans were living side by side."

Acheson's brow creased, giving the impression that he was considering Georgia's assumption. "Not at all, but it's interesting and we cannot simply dismiss that such overlapping stratigraphies are purely accidental."

"But you haven't found any dinosaurs," Phoebe Pack said. She was the second wife of Arthur Pack, the owner of the Ghost Ranch. "Our kids would have loved that!" The first wife of Pack had disappeared with the children's tutor but not the children. And it was nice, Georgia thought, that Phoebe now seemed to regard those three kids as hers as well as Arthur's. They needed an attentive mother and Phoebe was certainly that.

"No, no indeed. No dinosaurs." Acheson laughed.

Phoebe now turned to Georgia. "So, you're joining this expedition along with Orville Cox?"

"Not exactly," Georgia said. "Ansel and David and I are not digging for pottery or bone; we're just doing photography and painting in one of my favorite places. I call it the Black Place. It's about one hundred miles from here, north and west—the Bisti Lands, or Badlands is their more popular name. One of my favorite locations for painting. Amazing geological formations." She paused for a moment. "They are visually . . . well . . . just stimulating. You can imagine so much. Like reading cloud pictures, you know. I look at a cloud and might see a gazelle leaping across the sky and you see the Creation of Adam in the Sistine chapel." *Or maybe*, Georgia thought, *you see a prehistoric artist carving a prehistoric design with the dropped tooth of a mastodon who had both trod the earth at the same time.*

Phoebe seemed entranced by what Georgia had just said.

"Have you been to Rome, Georgia?"

"Not yet, but someday. Can't say I'm too fond of Mussolini at the moment. I hear that he is about to pass some racial laws just as Germany has."

"But would that affect you? Are you Jewish?" Phoebe asked.

Oh dear, Georgia thought to herself. She really liked Phoebe but she wasn't the sharpest blade in the cupboard.

"My husband is Jewish, but even if he weren't Jewish, yes. I think it affects all of us whether we are Jewish or not," Georgia replied simply.

A light seemed to flicker in Phoebe's pale blue eyes. "Why yes, I suppose you're right." She paused for a few seconds. Then with more force she said, "You are absolutely right. I regret that I said that." She then turned to McAlpin.

"And you, Mr. McAlpin? What is your interest?" Phoebe asked.

"Photography, but make no mistake, I'm strictly an amateur. However, I am involved in starting a photography center at Princeton. And Ansel here is donating several of his photographs."

"Mr. McAlpin—" Phoebe began to ask a question.

"David, please."

"David then, is it true that Albert Einstein is at Princeton?"

"Oh yes, very much so. He's been at Princeton for almost four years now. Let's say he left Germany as fast as he could, before any racial laws were passed. I think within days of Hitler becoming chancellor, or whatever the title is for a lunatic leader of the German Reich. Einstein is now at the Institute for Advanced Studies."

"Does he teach, or simply do research?" Acheson asked.

"Not exactly either, I believe," McAlpin replied. "He thinks . . . thinks with other thinkers about questions."

"And what exactly does that mean, Institute for Advanced Studies?" Arthur Pack asked.

"Well, I am the last person you should ask. I can't exactly understand what they do, but the best description I can give is that it is a center for speculation about the universe. So, if he teaches anything it's how to speculate about the universe, time, and the foundational elements of our existence." He paused at this point and looked at Acheson. "Not at all like your studies of tracing artifacts of previous cultures back in time. Time for Einstein is not exactly countable as I understand it. It's relative and never absolute, but it becomes very pronounced when approaching the speed of light." He inhaled deeply, then chuckled. "And that, my friends, is about the limit of my comprehension of what Einstein is doing. So please don't ask me any more questions, because I am definitely not a physicist, and I feel that the time you are speaking about, Professor Acheson, is much less abstract.

"An ancient potter making a pot and overlapping with a mastodon—that is by far more comprehensible." He paused. "And if this radiocarbon dating comes through, maybe it will be possible to pinpoint that kind of time, relative to when such creatures and humans might have existed together here in the southwest."

The following morning, McAlpin, Acheson, Ansel, Georgia, and Orville left in three pickup trucks before first light. Acheson and his assistant, Gideon Blake, a graduate student from Yale, were in one pickup going to their archaeology site. McAlpin and Ansel were in a second one, and Georgia and Orville were together in the third pickup.

Georgia studied Orville as he was driving. The sun began to slide in through the car window, casting his face in a warm light. She loved this man's face. It seemed as corrugated as the landscape and now, burnished in the reddish light of the dawn, it became a country unto itself.

"Whatcha thinking about, Orv?" Georgia asked.

"What you told me that fellow Acheson said last night—about the mastodons and the potsherds from the earliest Anasazi period, or even before."

"Yeah, something, isn't it? I picture them all sitting around in a kiva, the first people, the mastodon included, smoking a little peyote," Georgia said.

"Ha!" Orville slapped his knee. "And what would they be discussing, Georgia?"

"Not sure—maybe human evolution." She paused. "Maybe the ice age. When was that? Twenty thousand years ago, or so?"

"Round about then, I s'pose. Maybe even earlier," Orville answered.

Georgia looked out the car window. The landscape was changing, the colors shifting from rugged reds and browns into ashy grays. She could almost feel that molten energy rising from the earth as its innards had liquified millions of years ago and roiled into bubbling dark swells. A silent sea rising and collapsing into the soft dark hills that were now appearing on the horizon. *What a strange country this is*, she thought. Somber and mysterious. A lonely feeling place, as she had described it to Stieglitz. But Georgia knew he did not quite understand her penchant for such places. And this particular place had baffled him when she had described it. Nonetheless, he loved her paintings of the Black Place and was thrilled she was going back to what she sometimes called The Faraway. Yes, so unlike the places that Stieglitz was drawn to. He loved cauldrons of bubbling people and family and social life. The summer house on Lake George could be exhausting in her mind, as could his gallery, An American Place. But Georgia had a bent toward the infinite and the mystery of these badlands. *Bad girl on the loose*, she thought to herself and gave a laugh.

"What's so funny?" Orville asked.

"Oh, nothing much, just thinking about Stieglitz and how he'd hate this place." She paused. "He loves my paintings from here but would hate actually being here."

Orville had long ago stopped thinking about Georgia and her relationship with her husband, Alfred Stieglitz. He knew she had something going on with Sheriff McCaffrey. Other people might suspect as well, but people didn't butt into other people's business out here. That's just the way it was.

Georgia continued to gaze out the window at the ancient riverbeds coursing through the terrain like veins. There was a luminous quality to the land that spoke of an existence that was out of human grasp. And although she called it The Faraway, she wanted to grasp it. To paint it, to celebrate and honor its enigmatic and haunting origins of time and earth. In Georgia's mind, this Faraway was the marrow of the land, and somewhat ironically where many of the best bones she painted came from.

"I forgot to mention to you, Orville. I need to look up a friend in Far Cry while you're getting the horses out. I won't be long."

"Oh yes, your friend—the bone man lives near there, right?"

"Indeed, Juan Nez. He finds me the best bones. And I want to see if he has anything for me. There are a lot of mule deer around. They have the most fantastic antlers. They grow from a central antler then they fork off and make the most amazing geometries."

"You know what you are, Georgia?"

"What's that, Orv?"

"A hoarder. A hoarder of images."

"I don't have to own them. Not to worry. I won't be one of those little old ladies whose attic ceiling collapses and buries them under a ton of junk." She sighed. "I travel light."

Orville smiled and looked over at her. "Yes, you do, my dear. You travel light. No baggage."

"Oh, I got plenty of baggage. It's just that no one can see it."

Half an hour later they pulled up to the trading post in Far Cry.

THREE

Georgia jumped out of the car as soon as they parked. "I'll go in here and check on Juan's whereabouts," she said as Orville began to unload the horses to ride into wherever they decided to pitch their tents. "I'll just be a minute."

Georgia entered the trading post and was warmly greeted by the owner, Lucille Samuels.

"Where have you been, Georgia?"

"Well, pretty busy, but now I'm back to my favorite painting spot ever."

"You need to build a house out there before all the land gets eaten up by investors."

"Who's doing the eating?"

"Real-estate folks."

"But it's protected, isn't it?"

"The Navajo part, but that's all."

"This will be a disaster for archaeologists," Acheson said, walking into the trading post. "I can just imagine American millionaires building those Frank Lloyd Wright type houses all over the place and next there will be golf courses. It'll be the Palm Beach of the desert."

"I seriously doubt that." Georgia laughed. Her sister Anita, who had married a very wealthy man, had just bought a home in Palm Beach. Trying to imagine Anita in the Bisti Badlands was impossible.

"Hello there, Wynnie! At least I think that's you behind that stack of boxes you're carrying," Acheson called out. The young woman peered around the boxes and smiled.

Once again Georgia was stunned by Wynnie Haloke's beauty. Her earthy skin tone and high sculpted cheekbones set off her dark eyes. She was tall for a Navajo woman and had a regal bearing.

"Is Juan out back?" Georgia asked.

A worried look crossed Lucille's face.

"What's wrong?" Georgia asked. "Something happen to Juan?"

"Not sure," Lucille said. "He went off and hasn't been back." She sighed. "But he does this sometimes. Always complaining that Far Cry is getting too crowded. This place, crowded. Ha!" She turned now to Acheson. "So, Professor Acheson. What can I do for you?" Lucille asked.

"Well, a case of that canned milk would be good, and whatever else I had on that list."

"In other words, your standing order. I got it all packed and ready to go."

"Terrific."

"Wynnie," Lucille called to the back of the store where the young woman had just disappeared. "Can you get Professor Acheson's order?"

"Sure thing, Mam."

"What would you do without her?" Acheson asked.

"I don't know. She's not just tall, which I am not. So, she can reach anything. But she's smart. Took her just one hour to learn how to do the books."

"Smart as she is pretty," he commented.

Georgia winced a bit. It suggested that one could not be both, or that it was an unusual or freakish event. But she was worried about Juan. He knew she was coming. She had actually called the trading post and told Lucille to tell him to expect her.

"I've asked Wynnie to come out and work on the dig a bit. She did last year and she was great. Very meticulous. I hope you don't mind, Lucille."

"Not at all, Professor Acheson. I can always get one of her cousins in here to help out."

Georgia instantly forgave Acheson.

"What a nice idea, Professor," Georgia said. "That will give her something interesting for her résumé."

"I don't know if she is thinking in those terms. She talks about being a fishing guide."

"You mean working here at the trading post isn't enough?" Lucille interjected. "She's chief accountant and head of inventory management."

"That's exactly why she will be so good at helping us out. We need an excavation recorder. Every artifact must be recorded as to the layer in the stratigraphy in which it was found. The exact strata noted, a description of the trench it was found in, the context in short. That includes the soil matrix, the compaction of that matrix. Wynnie is a quick learner. She helped us out last year when we were in a pinch. So glad to have her back."

"Yes," Lucille offered. "She is meticulous. Did you know that she's a talented fly fisher too? She even makes the flies herself. I carry them here." She pointed at a rack that displayed various flies. Georgia walked over to look at them. They were quite beautiful. They hung from the rack like a swarm of alluring fairies.

"Beautiful," Georgia whispered. But nevertheless, the notion of Juan just disappearing gnawed at the back of her brain.

There was now the sound of a car pulling up.

"Must be Regina," Lucille remarked.

"Regina!" Acheson shouted. He bounded out of the trading post and sprinted toward the limousine.

"At last!" he cried as a statuesque woman of about Georgia's age stepped out of the limo. "Regina, my darling . . ." He embraced her.

"Dougie!" She exclaimed. "I'm the only one allowed to call him Dougie." She turned and appeared to announce this to the whole of Far Cry, all two hundred inhabitants. Only three of which were in the street now. It seemed as if the woman was putting a stamp on the archaeologist, a brand to announce her ownership to the world. Lucille was looking out the window.

"Yes, she has arrived!" she said, as if announcing a dignitary of some sort.

"Who is she?" Georgia asked.

"Regina Phelps. Professor Acheson's angel."

"Angel?"

"She funds all his work out there." Lucille sighed and wiped down a counter. "She's a Phelps as in the tires."

"The tires?"

"Yeah, you know, Phelps Everlasting Tires."

"Oh those. Yes. I've heard of them."

"Heard of them? You probably have Phelps tires on your car."

"Maybe, I don't know. I'm very ignorant about automobiles," Georgia replied. "Does she come out here often when the professor is digging?"

"Once or twice, but I guess he's found something pretty important. It's getting harder because the Navajo council is getting stricter about where people can dig."

"Think she'd be interested in any real estate?" Tommy Tso asked as he walked in the door. "So she can keep a closer eye on her 'investment'?" He was tall and lean, movie-star handsome, and undeniably charming. He had a small scar that interrupted his left eyebrow as if a fragment of lightning streaked through. It did not mar his handsome face. If anything, it conferred upon him a singular dignity.

"You mean Professor Acheson?" Lucille laughed. "You're a realtor, after all, Tommy."

"I sure am—off the reservation, of course. But I'll tell you to the east, close to the Colorado border, there's some fine land there. No archaeological sites, at least not so far. So, get it while you can. You interested, Miss O'Keeffe?"

"Not at all. A while back I bought my casita down on the Ghost Ranch. I don't need any more property out here." Stieglitz would be in a rage if he knew she had bought anything else. It took him months to calm down after she bought the casita.

"Any word about Juan?" Tommy asked. Lucille and Wynnie shook their heads.

"Georgia O'Keeffe! As I live and breathe." The tall woman who minutes ago had stepped out of the limousine swept into the trading post. She wore a cape and slim fitting pants with expensive cowboy boots. "When Dougie told me you were out here, I nearly died. As you know, I'm the owner of the Jack-in-the-Pulpit painting, number four. It hangs in my garden room on my horse farm in Virginia, and then the divine White Birch with those wonderful, delicious yellows is in the dining room. I could eat that painting. I love all those paintings. As you might know, my late husband's nickname was Jack."

Now, why would I know that? Georgia thought. This woman assumed a lot.

"That's why I bought it, the Jack-in-the-Pulpit one. And God knows he'd never been in a pulpit. But you know I look at that painting and I imagine his face."

She tipped her head to one side and closed her eyes as though she were imagining her late husband. Georgia knew she should take this as a compliment, but she was just trying to figure out how she got from a Jack-in-the-Pulpit to her husband. What features could they possibly share? She understood when people talked about, or more accurately wrote about, the similarities between some of her flower paintings and female genitalia. It was mostly male art critics. They became obsessed with the erotica in her paintings. One critic called them a "morphological metaphor" for female anatomy. *Reductive thinking*, she thought, then blinked as she tried to think of what Mr. Phelps, the Tire King as he was called, might look like that her Jack-in-the-Pulpit painting would remind his wife of him. *Actually*, she thought, *the flower did in fact possess a tall stalk with a sort of hood on top*. So, was it a phallus with a condom? Hardly female genitalia. Well, to each her own. If she wanted to plunk down twenty thousand dollars for a sexy flower, so be it.

Georgia blinked. This was not the visual transubstantiation that she had hoped for—some millionaire's face poking out of those dark, unfolding petals of the flowers.

Regina's words were alarming in some way. Perhaps it was never good to come face to face with a person who had bought one of her paintings. Now the woman was going on about the White Birch painting. Georgia had loved all the Lake George paintings, for the experience of painting them was so special in the fall when the leaves were just turning. It was like a palette unfolding before her eyes. For the White Birch she had been inspired by her sunrise rowboat trips on the lake. The foliage was a soft buttery yellow at that time of year.

Regina sighed. "The birches." She seemed to swoon at the thought. "I just love them, that yellow is yummy." Her tongue flicked out between her carefully painted lips. "I actually want my boudoir in my New York apartment painted in that color." Who used the word "boudoir" anymore? "So, I took the painting from my home in Virginia and shipped it to New York so my interior decorator could copy the color. I don't think he got it quite right. I might have to bring it back."

Oh don't! Georgia wanted to say. *Please don't.* But she said nothing. Regina kept chattering breathlessly. How the painting was like a fairyland, those woods with the birches. How she felt the wind in the trees; how the trees were like prayers, silent prayers. With every word the painting was dissolving in Georgia's mind. Why had she ever agreed to sell it? But twelve years ago, it was a staggering amount of money. She was never really that interested in who bought her paintings, and now she knew why. This woman who stood before her was growing more grotesque by the second. She hated to think of one of her paintings in any one of her many houses. The paintings suddenly seemed to Georgia like misplaced orphans. They needed to be rescued.

She had to say something. She needed to respond in some manner, some way, but she was at a loss. She mumbled a few words and was thankful that at that moment Tommy, who had briefly left, walked back through the door.

"Hello, beautiful," he called out. Regina whirled around.

"Tommy! Tommy Tso . . . Oh my goodness, as handsome as ever."

Tommy spread his arms wide. "Shall we, Regina?"

"Oh, darling!" she exclaimed, and they began a waltz of sorts around the trading post. "Takes me back to when you visited Bridlemere in Virginia."

Georgia noticed Wynnie in a corner at the back of the store. She was looking daggers at the dancing couple.

Georgia turned and walked a few steps over to Lucille. "So how long has Juan been gone, exactly?" she asked.

"Good question," Lucille said. "He's been away for a couple of days, maybe longer. I think he may have gone over to Chama where his sister lives." She paused and turned around as if to look over her shoulder, then lowered her voice. "There is one little boy, Pablo, who is very upset."

"Pablo Jemez?" Georgia asked. "That nice little boy who helps him clean the bones?"

"Yes, Juan is his godfather or whatever the Navajos call it. He helps the old man with everything. They are very close. Not sure if there's a blood connection or what."

"Where is Pablo now?"

"Out back, near the stables. He could use some cheering up."

"I'll go see him."

Georgia walked out toward the stables.

"Pablo!" she called out. There was no answer. She went inside. Her shadow slid across the stalls. There was the sound of a horse snorting and then the thump of its hooves.

"Pablo, child, where are you?" She saw a hunched figure ahead crouched beside a dismantled wagon. "Pablo, is that you? And there's Diablo, I see."

He was in front of a cage holding the trading post's pet Gila monster. Pablo appeared to be about to slide a plump barn mouse into the cage. The blue forked tongue of the lizard unfurled, anticipating the mouse. The Gila monster was a formidable-looking creature, despite its small size. Its scales resembled an intricate black and pinkish beadwork design. It reminded her of some slippers she had bought at the Taos pueblo. The lizard opened his jaws and sunk his fangs in the mouse. "Down the hatch," Georgia said. She could see the bulge in the lizard's midsection as it went down.

"You want to hold him?" Pablo asked. "I have gloves. You have to wear gloves 'cause they have a mean bite."

"No thank you, Pablo."

The boy stood up and sniffled. "Juan knows how to handle them. They never bite him. He doesn't even have to wear gloves." He paused and seemed to just stare into space, then turned his attention to Georgia. "As a matter of fact, Juan knew how to hypnotize them."

"What?"

"Yep, he did. But I can't do it."

"You tried?"

"Once, but I was too scared. See, you have to get down, and look them straight in their eyes, then quickly flip them. They don't move fast at all. They are really slow. But if they look in your eyes they sort of freeze—kind of like hypnotizing them—then you flip them over so they stay like that." He sighed. "Juan was really good at it."

"I came looking for Juan. He said he might have some bones for me." She paused. "He's not here, I understand." Pablo shook his head wearily.

"How long has he been gone?"

"A few days."

"A few days doesn't seem such a long time. What about Pedro?" she asked, referring to Juan's burro.

"He's gone too." They both continued watching the Gila monster as it digested the barn mouse. "You see." Pablo pointed at the lizard whose jaws were still moving. "They store the poison back here." He pointed at his own neck. "In these muscles."

"Muscles?"

"Not exactly muscles. I forget what they call them."

"Glands?"

"Yeah, that's the word. The venom is back there in the lower part of its jaw. And they connect with its teeth which have grooves in them that help get the poison, it just pumps it in." He was quiet for several seconds as they watched the creature.

"You know the story, Miss O'Keeffe, about Coyote and the lizards?"

"Don't believe I do."

"It's one of those stories, you know, what do you call them . . . not in the Bible like the priests talk about, the other kind."

"Legend? Myth?"

"Yeah, I guess so. A tale like a legend. Very old. Maybe true, maybe not, but believed."

"Oh yes, those are the best kind."

"You know how Coyote is. He is very curious and loves to spy on other creatures. So, one day he saw a bunch of lizards sliding down the side of a small hill on flat rocks. Coyote wanted to play. But the lizards did not like that idea.

"'Please,' the coyote said. 'It seems like a lot of fun. You're having such a good time. What do you call your game?'

"'We just call it sliding.'

"'You are not a lizard,' one of them said. 'Go play your own games. You don't know ours.'

"'But I can learn,' Coyote said. 'Really, it looks very easy.'

"'This game is very dangerous. You'd get killed,' an old lizard told him.

"Coyote didn't believe a word of that. None of the lizards had been hurt, so why should he? He kept begging them to let him try it, just once.

"'Well, just once, cousin,' said the oldest lizard after hearing Coyote begging. 'You can ride the small flat rock, but don't ask to ride the big one.'

"But Coyote didn't listen to them, and he climbed onto the big rock. And he soon tumbled from it and saw that the big rock would squash him now. 'I should have listened,' he thought. 'I'm going to be smashed flat by the big rock, just as they said.'

"The lizards stood looking down at him. 'Poor, foolish Coyote,' the oldest lizard said. 'He's no friend of mine, but still it makes me sad to see him smashed so flat.'

"'And right in the middle of our runway,' said one of the young lizards. 'It would serve him right to leave him there.'

"'He's going to be very heavy for us to move,' said another.

"'It would be simpler to bring him back to life,' said a third lizard. 'Then he could leave without us having to move him.'

"'You have a very good idea,' said the oldest lizard. 'Come on, friends.'

"One at a time they slid down to Coyote and made a circle

around him so they could work their magic. And in their own secret way, they brought him back to life.

"'Now go on your way, Coyote,' the oldest lizard told him. 'And after this, don't try to play lizard games again. We are our own kind.'

"Coyote was glad to be alive again. He got up and dashed for home as fast as he could run."

"Hmm," said Georgia. "Do you think Coyote listened after that?"

"Probably not. Coyote never listens. Too proud to listen."

"Some people are like that too," Georgia said. And they continued to crouch side by side, watching the Gila monster.

"So," Georgia murmured softly as they watched, "where do you think Juan and Pedro could have gone?"

"I dunno. Tommy went looking for him, but couldn't find him or Pedro."

"Tommy Tso went?"

Pablo nodded.

"Tommy's your cousin, isn't he?"

He nodded again. Pablo himself was an orphan, and the responsibility of his upbringing seemed to be traded around the many members of his family. The Tso branch were people of the Towering House clan. Tommy was the pride of the family for he had graduated with a law degree from the University of Colorado law school and was very involved with land rights for the Navajo people. The Diné was the term that the Navajo used to refer to themselves and it meant The People.

"I have a bad feeling, Miss O'Keeffe," Pablo said, turning his head away from Diablo.

Georgia patted his shoulder.

"Well, let's not panic." *What a stupid thing to say*, she thought.

"But, Miss O'Keeffe, he's an old man. And sometimes he has breathing problems."

"He's a tough old man, Pablo . . . and Pedro would have trotted back here if he was in any kind of trouble. He is so devoted to him."

"But Pedro's stupid. Really stupid. When it rained really hard here last spring, he stood outside with his mouth open looking at the sky. He would have drowned if my uncle hadn't brought him inside."

Georgia sighed.

Pablo stood up. "You want to look at the bones?"

"Sure, if you have any."

"He always has some for you, Miss O'Keeffe." He paused. "Just one mule deer's antlers, but he was sure he'd find some more on this trip. And there are some others in the back here that you might like."

There were four or five horse skulls, a few pelvises, and a lot of antlers from elk and pronghorn as well as another smaller horse skull that was quite handsome, and as promised a set of mule deer antlers. It was difficult to orient the position of the mule deer's. If they were forward facing it meant that the creature was more of a sheep and not an antelope, and this seemed to be the case. As she looked through the large crate with the bones, it seemed to her that there was something more alive about the bones than seeing the animal in life, walking about or leaping across the desert in graceful arcs. The bones were strangely animated. There was a keenness to them, a fervor that expressed a kind of essence of life. But almost paradoxically there was an abstract quality to the bones that enticed her. She loved the spaces created by the bones. The eye sockets, the pelvic apertures of the skeletons of dead horses served as frames for grasping the world. To view the sky, the universe through the portal of a bone was an entirely new way to look at what was around one. Negative space intrigued Georgia.

Of course, what she was really hoping for was a spectacular rack of antlers from a mule deer. The one he found was from a not-quite-full-grown one. Juan had promised her he would find a big one; that there was a place that many passed when they shed their antlers in the winter and that he would go there this summer.

There was one skull in the pile of bones that Pablo led her to that had been bleached to a white intensity that was absolutely dazzling.

She turned to Pablo. "These are all wonderful. I think right now that I'll just take this horse skull. It is so elegant. I can really imagine setting it on some of the black rocks out there. I'll come back for the rest at the end of our trip and take them back to the Ghost Ranch, but just this one for now."

"Yá'át'ééh." A voice came from behind them.

"Adá'í," Pablo immediately cried out. "You found him?"

Tommy strode into the barn and shook his head. "No, sorry. But, Pablo, don't give up hope. He's a tough old codger, that one."

Georgia now realized what a handsome fellow Tommy really was. Tall for a Navajo. Wide forehead with slightly sloping dark eyes. He turned to Georgia. "You hoping for bones, Miss O'Keeffe?"

"Nice dance you had there at the trading post," she replied.

"Ah yes, Mrs. Phelps," he said somewhat dismissively, or perhaps it was apologetically. "So, did you find some nice bones out here?" he asked again.

"Yes, Juan collects them for me."

"Hope he doesn't charge you too much." He smiled.

"Not a penny sir," Georgia replied.

"That is so like Juan." Tommy put his hands around Pablo's shoulders and brought him close to his side. "And this young fellow is missing him, something fierce. Right, Pablo?"

"Right, Tommy," Pablo muttered.

"But I keep telling him that Juan is tough, tough as old leather. He knows the Badlands like the back of his hand."

"That's what worries me," Pablo said. "Just that. He never gets lost."

"I'll send my guys out again. I promise." He then turned to Georgia. "Nice to have you here again, Miss O'Keeffe. And maybe someday I'll be able to afford one of your paintings."

Georgia hated it when people mentioned anything to do with the price of her paintings. It seemed especially crude to change the subject from Pablo's beloved godfather to money. And the words "my guys" annoyed her too. She watched Tommy as he walked almost daintily across the corral. That's when she noticed his boots. Fancy, expensive boots. Stetson boots, undoubtedly, more than fifty dollars a pair. This town of Far Cry was dirt poor. Tommy Tso did not belong here, but rather on a dude ranch wooing young debutantes from the east.

FOUR

The ride out to their campsite was always the favorite part of arriving at Far Cry. The last color was draining from the sky, and it felt as if Georgia was discarding the world behind her and gradually immersing herself in this odd but wonderful landscape. The air was different here. A coolness had settled across the land. She felt as if she were being absorbed into the countryside. The deepening lavender of the evening wrapped around her. Soon it would be pitch black. She wanted to feel the darkness as it swallowed the day, feel the lavender of the night as it teetered on the brink of blackness. No matter that she was chilly now. She was sentient. Every molecule of life seemed to be touching her.

"Don't!" she called out to McAlpin, who had just turned on a flashlight.

"You can see all right, Georgia?"

"I can see fine. I see our campsite already. Lucille's cousin always sets it up for us, complete with a fire pit dug for cooking."

"By golly, you have good eyes," McAlpin commented. "I guess you should." He chuckled.

"Not any better than yours. I'm just good at shredding this desert light."

"Shredding not shedding?"

Georgia laughed. "Yes, shredding. See, I can tell you're looking directly at the setting sun, but I'm looking just slightly below it. And I can see the shadows of the tents that Lucille's cousin pitched for us. And you will too. Just get used to it, and you will see even more." She paused. "You'll see better."

"But I'm not a painter. I just work in photography. Only black and white."

"You'll see black and white better. I promise you," Georgia replied.

She heard Ansel laugh. "She's right, David."

By the time they had arrived at their camp, the stars had broken out.

McAlpin and Orville turned in for the night in their respective tents. Georgia and Ansel sat by the last embers of the campfire and watched the stars climbing into the sky. There was just enough light to see the hills rising in the east like the march of distant elephants. Beneath the footfalls of the elephants were layers upon layers of time, of earth's history. There were eroding rocks that formed a palette of inky blacks, then an odd, deeper black with a hint of navy blue, then the ashy gray that almost rumbled with an echo of ancient volcanoes.

Georgia's task was to sort out the grays from the almost grays and the fathomless blacks from the near blacks. "Sifting" was the word that came to her mind. *I am sifting particles of a spectrum, a dark spectrum, and yes, one of time.* The skin of the night was forming. She tipped her head back as the dark quenched the last scraps of the day, revealing more and more stars. The galaxies, magnificent in their silent gyrations, disclosing another kind of light in the vastness of the dark sky.

A magazine writer had once asked her what her first memory was and, without hesitation, she said the brightness of light. She swore she was only about eight or nine months old at the time when, on a very dark winter day, a blade of sunlight cut through the shadows, and she became absolutely gleeful. She had been sitting on pillows atop a patchwork quilt that was white with red stars. It was as if the red of those stars poured through her. She turned now to Ansel.

"Do you remember the first picture you ever took?"

"The first picture I took or wanted to take?"

"Well, wanted to take."

"I was sick in bed with a cold. I was about twelve years old, and my Aunt Mary gave me a book—*In the Heart of the Sierras* was the title. I was instantly enthralled, and I convinced my parents that we had to go there. So as soon as I was better, my father gave me a Kodak Box Brownie camera. We went to Yosemite, and I climbed up an old disintegrating tree stump and took my first picture of Half Dome." He laughed. "The stump is all gone, but I'm still here and I'll go back to Yosemite in the fall, and take God knows what—my one thousandth picture of Half Dome? But this is pretty fine out here." He nodded and tipped his head toward the sky.

"That it is," Georgia whispered. She sighed. "I'm worried about Juan."

"Juan, your bone man?"

"Yes, he knows this country like the back of his hand. I . . . I . . . I hate to think of him hurt or dying out here, the animals picking on his bones." She laughed harshly. "I know that sounds funny in a way, because of my own attraction to bones. But you know the animal bones that I find are strangely more alive to me than the animals themselves walking around with their tails switching." She sighed. "Sorry to be so morbid."

"He is your friend, Georgia. Don't be so hard on yourself."

She got up. "Time to turn in. Gotta catch that dawn light against the elephants."

And she would dream that night of elephants marching along the crest of the distant hills. Their shadows lifelike, trying to catch up with their corporeal beings and not linger as mere shadows against the light.

She was eager to start the day. She imagined squeezing out paints from the tubes onto her palette. A ravenous hunger came over her, as it often did when she conjured up the sensation of squeezing paint from a tube. She wanted to eat it – eat it more than the bacon that Orville would be cooking in the skillet over the campfire when she woke.

Just before dawn, Ansel came out from his little canvas dark-room.

"Look what I got here!" he called to Georgia when he saw her.

The print was still dripping with fixer as he walked toward her. "I caught the morning star. And what did you catch, Georgia?"

She was sitting on a camp stool. In her lap was a cow skull which she was caressing with one hand.

"Just found this over there, fifty feet from my tent." She nodded in the direction. "Juan must have missed it, although I think he knew this was one of my favorite campsites. Such a beauty, this one."

"So, the bones are coming to you?" Ansel said.

"Maybe. You catch the stars, and I catch the bones." She sighed and thought of Juan.

FIVE

Twenty minutes later, Orville Cox strode toward Georgia as she was arranging her painting gear into saddlebags on her horse, Dottie.

"I'll go with you and be your caddy," Orville said as Georgia tightened the belts for the gear. The pinto was her favorite horse from the Ghost Ranch, the one that she always rode on painting expeditions that took her into rough country where her Model A could not go.

"My caddy." Georgia laughed. "Orville, did I ever tell you about the time I attempted to play golf with Stieglitz's sister Selma?"

"Is she the bossy one?"

"Understatement of the year. Yes, that's the one. So bossy. But one day I almost inadvertently killed her dog with my golf ball."

"You're kidding?"

"Nope, not at all and not intentionally. The dog was a loathsome, yappy creature. Selma insisted on taking that dog with her everywhere. She claimed I intended to kill him. But the dog had run out onto the green. I was so excited that my ball was even headed for that green and was on target for the hole—you know, with a flag on the pole. Me getting a hole in one! Imagine that! But then I saw that the flagpole seemed to suddenly bend and there was this fuzzy white heap next to it. It was Rippy, Selma's cairn terrier."

"Did he die?"

"No, unfortunately."

"Why was the dog let on in the first place?"

"Obviously you don't know Alfred's sister Selma. She is a force of nature."

"Well, so are you, Georgia."

"She tried to get me banned from the golf course because

of that. Claimed I was a danger to the club. A dangerous lady. A hazard to the other players."

Orville chuckled. "You are in your own way, Georgia."

"What way is that, Orv?"

"Hard to describe."

"Try."

"You see things others don't, Georgia. That is a force you have."

"Hmmph." She often made that sound when dismissing an argument. "Well, obviously I didn't see that idiotic dog chasing my golf ball to the eighth green at the Quinniponek Golf Club."

"That's the name of the golf club? Sounds Indian."

"Yep. That's the name. A lot of things are named after Indians but of course Indians are not allowed to join the club."

After a while, Orville halted his horse and stood up in his stirrups, scanning the landscape. "Let's stop just ahead. We're heading toward Hoodoo Ville."

A quarter mile or so ahead, the terrain was punctuated by a cluster of hoodoos, the thin spires of twisted rock formations sculpted by wind and erosion. They pierced the sky like desert skyscrapers.

"We'll get some shade there later this morning when they start to cast shadows."

"Good idea."

Ten minutes later they began to unpack the gear—the painting equipment and items Orville had brought for "morning tea," as he called it. Georgia would paint there until mid-morning and then they would return to camp as the heat and the sun would become unbearable. There was nothing crueler out here in The Faraway than the sun from mid-morning until mid-afternoon. It was like Hell's waiting room.

Georgia turned toward the east and her eyes settled on an extraordinary collision of two dark hills. There was something about this silent crash of the black and the grays that reminded her—of all things—of amaryllis petals. She had painted the opening stages of the flower last winter as someone had sent her a bulb that began to bloom, unfurling its petals in late

January. The species was called Red Lion. Every day as it opened its petals the flower seemed to unlock into a new configuration and now, here in the Black Place, she was seeing a counterpart in eroding rock—grays and whites unfolding like petals of time and erosion. When she painted the Red Lion amaryllis she felt as though she were capturing the immensity of the flower, and now it was as though flower and rock had combined to suggest the immensity of time.

It was so peaceful out here. The only sound was the occasional neighs of their horses and then, every once in a while, the whisper of a breeze.

Georgia caught sight of Orville, his long legs striding across the desert, his head bowed. He carried a stick and poked at things. He was looking for a special kind of rock that he called Apache Tears. His niece was a jeweler in Santa Fe, and she loved the smooth, jet-black pebbles that were formed from volcanic glass. She made beautiful necklaces from them. Orville stopped and waved his hat to fan his face.

"Georgia, it's getting hot out there. Time to pack up. I don't want you keeling over on me."

"I've never keeled over on anybody. But yes, time to quit."

As she turned around to pack up her easel, she noticed that the hoodoos had cast a latticework of shadows on the ground. It could almost be a prison. A prison of shadows. *What a peculiar place this is*, she thought. There was so much to paint here, a place that most people would think of as completely barren. She did not have to search for the austerity here. Everything was pared down so the shapes, the narrow range of colors, suddenly became rich in their very bleakness. It reminded Georgia of when she had finally figured out how to paint New York City. It had to be at night. That was when the city attained the graceful austerity of its glass and steel beauty. This was when its elegant geometry was completely revealed, and it was absolutely dazzling.

By the time they returned to the campsite, it was still too hot to be out under the blazing sun and the rest of the group had all retreated to their tents or unfurled their sunshades and were napping. But the images Georgia had seen kept her awake.

Tomorrow, she vowed to go to a place they had passed on the way back. She had made Orville stop while she quickly sketched it. It was so alive in her mind that she decided to write Stieglitz a letter about it. Cross-legged and bent over a sketching board, she began to write to him:

Dear One,

I am broiling here even under the sunshade of my tent but could not nap as I should in the middle of the day. Yes, I am in The Faraway—the Black Place that every hour seems to reveal something new to me. When I see this country in its dusty but silvery beauty and forbidding blackness, it is almost as if I see you too—your silver hair and gray clothes and black cape. The irony of this is amazing—that this austere place out in the middle of nowhere would conjure up thoughts of you. I have to laugh as I am certain that you would hate it here. Most likely the temperature is a hundred degrees or higher. A dry heat, however. And right now, as I look out my tent, I feel as if I can see the Forever here. Yes, the Forever in The Faraway! Such ironies beguile me.

Every day, I'm on the lookout for just the right bones—preferably a multiple pronged animal skull. It's difficult to explain how the bones in some way connect me with this notion of what I would call the Forever in The Faraway. When I find the right skull with a multitude of antlers, I shall place it directly on the ground. And then I must wait for the sky to look just right, no clouds. I just want the blue sky filling the spaces between the antlers or the eye sockets of a skull. That's when you truly see blue, when it is framed by the orifices of the bones. I don't need a skull or antlers specifically. Pelvis bones are terrific too. I plan to blend the spatial dimensions into a kind of melding of background—sky and the foreground with the bone into a single composition, or should I call it a narration? Of course, to do this I am violating all rules of composition. But as you have often said, I am a violator. So, onward! Must go, dear one.

P.S. Any news about Amelia Earhart? So shocking. I continue to hope for the best.

Suddenly there was the sound of horse hooves pounding the ground. Whoops and hollers seared the air. Two riders jumped from their horses. Orville stood up to greet them.

"What's up, Gideon? I take it there is something that is cause for celebration?" Orville asked.

Tall and rangy, the young man walked with a swagger and seemed quite jubilant. "Betcha fuckin' boots it's cause for celebration."

"Hey, there's ladies here!" Orville responded.

"Oh sorry. Miss O'Keeffe, I believe?" He said, turning to Georgia who had come out from her tent.

"That's all right. I haven't yet had the pleasure properly." She stepped forward and extended her hand.

"Gideon, Gideon Blake."

"Well, what brings you here in this excess of joy?" Ansel came forward and patted the flanks of Blake's horse. "A Clovis point?"

"Better, older."

"Older?" Orville asked.

"A pottery fragment. Really, two large fragments. Sacred bowls, very primitive. Professor Acheson guesses that they are twenty thousand years before present time, at least."

"What makes them sacred?" Georgia asked. *Age*, she wondered. If so, she might have a chance, she was tempted to say jokingly. But for archaeologists she knew that age was never a laughing matter.

"The designs. Very primitive versions of the symbols of what Professor Acheson calls the arc of life—kind of like a rainbow which brings the blessing of rain. This predates anything at Chaco Canyon." Chaco Canyon was, at this point in time, the site to beat amongst archaeologists. And Harvard seemed to be in the lead with their excavations. It was just another version of the Harvard-Yale football game, a rivalry that had been going on since 1875.

Blake looked at the group. "So, we'd like to invite you over tonight for a celebration. Our camp is not far from here, just a couple of miles or so. You should come and see the site. Professor Acheson even managed somehow to get a few bottles of champagne to celebrate." He paused. "I believe thanks to Mrs. Phelps."

"I'm always up for champagne," Ansel said.

"Sure," McAlpin replied.

Ansel turned to Georgia. "You in, Georgia?"

"Why not? But I can't promise I'll last long."

The distance was more like three miles, and it took about twenty-five minutes with the horses. Although Georgia had been reluctant to go as she was tired from the heat and sun, she found the ride refreshing. A cooling breeze had begun to blow. The night was cloudless and the moon almost full. The shadows of the horses as they rode blended into each other to make a multi-headed beast on the dried riverbed they were crossing, and stars were flung across the sky. She found the Pleiades. She recalled a story that Ryan had told her, a Navajo myth about the Black God who created the Pleiades. The Black God did it in an orderly fashion, but then Coyote came along and also wanted to place stars. So, Coyote just grabbed a pawful of stars and flung them into the night all helter-skelter. Coyote wasn't evil, really, but it did seem that the creature's main occupation was messing things up, creating chaos out of order.

As the group drew closer to the archaeology site, they could hear the merriment of the celebration spilling across the desert.

"How about it!" Douglas Acheson ran up to Orville and slapped his horse's shoulder. The animal spooked a bit and jumped sideways.

"Easy there, partner," Orville said and leaned over to calm the horse.

"Sorry, Orville, we are just all so excited. This is a monumental moment for our team. It's really a landmark in southwestern archaeology. Eat your heart out, Edmund Welles."

Georgia recognized the name. Welles was the Harvard archaeologist who was irrevocably linked to the Chaco Canyon ruins. Acheson's crew of graduate students were well into their cups by this time, celebrating the astounding discovery.

"Well," McAlpin said. "Can you show us what you've got?"

"Right this way, sir." Acheson made a gesture similar to that of a maître d' showing a valued customer to a table. They walked a few steps over to a blanket spread on the ground. Acheson sank to his knees and drew out a flashlight. "Come on. Get down here so you can see these gems." His flashlight played over the two fragments. One was at least eight inches across; the other about half that size. The markings were clearly visible.

"Rainbow arc, not as refined as the ones a thousand years later, but definitely indicative as a forerunner of the arc of life motifs associated with the Anasazi's most sacred sites."

"But if this is a sacred site," Orville said as his finger traced the perimeter of the fragment, "then the Navajo heritage group is going to raise hell. You know how they are about keeping sacred places sacred. They're trying right now to get laws passed to avoid contamination of sacred places."

"They call it contamination. I call it education. The more we learn about these places, the better we are going to care about them and be able to protect them," Acheson retorted.

"Mmm . . ." was Orville's only response. He was probably thinking about the oil that was discovered a decade before in Oklahoma, in the Osage territory. Indians got rich and then one by one they were being killed off. It was only eight years ago that J. Edgar Hoover got on the case and a man was charged with the murders. These ancient ruins, sacred places admittedly, were hardly equal to discovering the underground riches of oil, but Orville nevertheless sensed that there were some high stakes here. Was it a discovery equal to King Tut's tomb, which had been unearthed more than a dozen years before? Not by a long shot. But as ruins go, if this team uncovered an ancient kiva that predated all the others in the southwest, it would be big news. Every archaeologist across the country would come running. And how would the Navajos like that? There were precious few protections for their land.

Yes, there was Navajo Tribal Police, created in 1872. It had gone through many iterations and each one seemed to reduce its power and its reach. There were now fewer than fifty Navajo police officers spread over 27,000 square miles of the Navajo nation, and most likely none assigned to the Bisti Badlands. No banks, no stores, no livestock. The potential for crime was zero—unless one dug very deep. Then there might be history or oil. And if there was oil, well history be damned.

"And who was the lucky person who found it?" Orville asked.

"None other than our very own Wynnie Haloke!" Blake boomed. He went to the table where the champagne, paper cups, and snacks were set out. He grabbed Wynnie's hand and lifted a glass of champagne. "Here's to Wynnie and her sharp eyes! Three cheers for Wynnie!"

Wynnie tucked her chin and even through the golden-brown tint of her skin a blush crept up. She looked extremely uncomfortable.

"How'd you do it, Wynnie?" someone called out.

"Keen eyes," Blake snapped. "You could all take lessons from Wynnie. She probably found some small, almost sand grain-size fragments that somehow didn't feel right or stood out in some very subtle way from the sediment in the sifting screen. Was that it, Wynnie?"

"Sort of, I guess."

"Sort of, she guesses! Let's see your hands."

"Huh?" Wynnie asked. She clearly was perplexed by the request.

Blake grabbed her hand and held it up again. "Tender fingertips! Sensitive skin. She felt the difference, I would guess. That's why I always say don't wear gloves when you're excavating."

Georgia found this account, this display, uncalled for. She could see that Wynnie was mortified. It was as if her space was somehow being violated but all with good cheer and a rah-rah spirit. Her eyes were cast down. Poor thing, what was she thinking? Of course, it hadn't helped that Orville had questioned the possibility of contamination of sacred places.

Blake now held up his own hands. "No tender fingertips here. Grew up on a farm. Nothing like digging potatoes and shucking corn, wrestling pigs, repairing farm equipment to roughen up your hands."

"Are you suggesting," McAlpin said, "that Wynnie has never worked, and therefore her hands and fingertips are more sensitive than yours?"

"Course not. That gal's a hard worker. Every Indian is." The conversation was taking a turn that Georgia found not only unfathomable but disturbingly condescending. "But does this look like farm country to you?" Blake asked.

"No," McAlpin answered. "But you get your hands in the dirt all day as an archaeologist."

"Not the same. Try filing a hoof on a large plow animal. Or just digging in the dirt all day for potatoes. Now there's more modern equipment, but back when I was growing up it was bending over all day and digging with your hands. I was the first person in my town to go to college. No more potatoes for me. Can't stand to look at them. But digging for stories, now, that was my dream come true." He sighed. "However, my fingertips are too calloused to find any real gems. When you can't see the gems with your naked eye, you have to be able to feel them, and I can't." He wiggled his fingers in the air.

Georgia saw that Wynnie had moved away from Blake as he continued to expand on his humble beginnings with interjections from Acheson.

"Gideon came to Yale—what was it, five years ago? And now he's currently in a doctoral program that is funded by our generous friend Regina Phelps." There was a burst of applause. "Come here, Regina, take a bow."

"Oh, please," she said modestly. "My pleasure to help young people get a start."

The tall, elegant lady swept forward. She was stunningly dressed. No faded jeans for her, but the high-waisted slacks that the movie star Katharine Hepburn was often photographed wearing. Georgia had read in a fashion magazine that this style was now being called the "American Look": "relaxed," "unconstructed." To complete the look, Regina wore a tailored jacket casually draped over her shoulders with prominent shoulder pads. On her finger, somewhat in contrast to the casual look that she had cultivated, was one of the largest diamond rings Georgia had ever seen.

Georgia yawned and turned to Orville. "Time to go, I think. I want to get up before dawn. Before the sun eats the light," she said. For that was how she thought of the rising sun—the light eater. For an hour before dawn and for two hours after, the light was perfect out in the Black Place. After that point, everything began to broil—the sky, the air, the rocks, and the land. When she wasn't driving her car, she always brought a little pop-up tent to nap under until the light became decent again.

The whole group mounted up now, anxious to get back to their campsite and turn in. Each had their own agenda. McAlpin wanted to follow Ansel and see how he chased light. For Ansel, light was a treasure, as it washed over the dark masses of the Black Place. It animated the landscapes, gave them a life that, although fleeting, revealed nevertheless a luminous, inescapable insistence.

McAlpin recalled Ansel's words from the morning they went together out into the desert. McAlpin had been eager to photograph a petrified tree stump he had glimpsed that first morning. Just as he was about to take the picture, Ansel put his hand on his arm. "Wait!" he whispered as if disclosing a vital secret—which he was. "Wait for the shadow. Where light and shadow fall, that is the essence of your story. You're not out here *taking* pictures, you're here to *make* pictures. There's a narrative here. There's suspense."

Georgia was also thinking about light. In her mind, she had sequestered an entire portfolio of images from this day. She was thinking about the irony of this landscape; in a place of hard rock and erosion she was finding images that suggested suppleness and fluidity. The waves of the eroding hills that were buried a million years ago often rose like a dark, rolling sea. Or perhaps like the painting she had worked on today, where the ledges seemed to unfurl like the petals of a flower. How were these elements transformed in her mind into something so different, so incongruous with what they had been. For such a seemingly barren place, there was an excess of riches. One just had to be patient—patient with the light, patient for the shadows. They were all characters in an ever-unfolding drama.

As they rode back, Georgia and Orville were side by side. The moonlight splashed down on them. She looked at him. He was perhaps ten years older than herself. His face was incised with deep creases. Laughing creases, she often thought of them. For he often laughed and had the best smile in the world, but right now he was not laughing or smiling.

"What's up, Orville? You look . . . well, disturbed."

"I am disturbed."

"What about?"

"Those potsherds they were showing us. Carrying on with champagne and all."

"What's the problem? You think . . .?"

A slash of moonlight cut diagonally across his face. He halted his horse.

"You mean sacred lands?" she whispered.

He nodded.

"But, Orville, that dig site is not on sacred lands."

"You're right. It's not."

But Georgia could tell that Orville was still disturbed. Maybe, she thought, it wasn't exactly a cause for celebration with champagne and all. Were they being exploitative of these people's land, the Navajos' land? What did the Navajos get in return?

SIX

At half past six the following morning, Wynnie had set up her sifting tray and emptied the yield from grid #31, which they had not gotten to the previous day. She began to shake the grid box, sifting for any pieces as she reflected on Blake's remarks from last evening. "Tender fingertips, my ass," she muttered. Just as she was giving one last shake to the filtering screen before she would paw through the remnants that were left, she glimpsed what appeared to be a fragment of bone—no, not bone, but wood of some sort—petrified? It blended in perfectly. She picked it out, spit on it, and then rubbed it with her fingers. The piece was marked by a kind of swirled grain pattern. Her first thought was that it was a fragment of a cottonwood root. The root was often used in healing ceremonies. But a petrified piece of wood might suggest special powers and this piece had been worked by human hands in some way. But for what? Maybe a sand painting ceremony. A healing ritual that used plant or tree spirits. And why would it be here in this treeless place? Nothing here so far had suggested that where they were digging was or had been a kiva. If they had been excavating a kiva site, it might indicate that a kiva structure had been built here at one time. But they had dug down only a meter and had not yet encountered any building foundations. There was not a trace of stone masonry or adobe that suggested such a building had existed here.

"My goodness! Lost in thought!"

Wynnie jumped and nearly upset the screening box.

"Oh dear, I didn't mean to startle you," Regina Phelps said.

"Oh . . . oh . . . that's fine. I just didn't expect anyone to be up yet."

"Well, I am. But aren't you the diligent soul laboring before breakfast. You and Miss O'Keeffe. She told me these are her favorite hours when the light is just right for painting. But you're not painting."

"No, just looking . . . just sifting here."

"Find anything else as great as those pottery fragments you showed us last night?"

"Uh . . ." She hesitated. "Not really."

"Your magic fingertips aren't awake yet."

"There is nothing magic about my fingertips, Mrs. Phelps."

"Please just call me Regina."

"No magic, Regina." She gave a quick smile.

"I didn't think so. I think it was all diligence on your part." She paused for a moment. "I sensed you were uncomfortable with that fellow Orville's remarks about disturbing sacred sites."

Wynnie just shrugged but said nothing. Regina looked at her narrowly. "If there is anything that disturbs you, Wynnie, about this dig, I want to know. Even though I am not an expert by any means, as a benefactor I have a responsibility. A responsibility that I take very seriously."

"Yes, Mam." She looked up and gave a quick smile. "I mean Regina."

She could not help but wonder if this woman ever had any kind of responsibility. She oozed privilege. But then again, she didn't want to be too judgmental. "Want to help me here with the screening?"

"Of course; I was hoping someone would ask me to actually participate. Giving money is rather boring after all. I'd like to learn something."

"OK, just paw through this screen with me and see if you discover anything that looks like more than just dirt. If you do, let me know."

"Happy to help." She laughed softly. "Maybe I have magic fingertips like you. Fingertips that I can assure have certainly not dug potatoes or filed horses' hooves like Gideon Blake."

Wynnie almost gasped. So, the lady has a sense of humor. She looked up at her and gave a smile. "I would have never guessed," she replied with a big smile.

Regina stood at one side of the sifting box and Wynnie at the other.

"Reminds me of playing in the sand box when I was a little kid."

"You did that when you were little?" Wynnie asked.

"Don't most kids?"

"Maybe. I don't know."

"No sand boxes out here?"

"The whole country is one giant sand box," Wynnie said.

Regina laughed softly. "I suppose so." She paused. "Maybe we'll find a potsherd like the ones you found."

"I doubt it," Wynnie replied.

"Why?"

"That was weird," Wynnie said.

"Weird in what way?"

"Unexpected. I . . . I . . . hope we don't find another one."

"Well, why's that?"

"Those things are only found in sacred lands."

"But these aren't sacred lands. I know we must be very careful about that."

"Yes, yes we must."

How odd their hands appeared as they sifted through almost side by side. Regina's hands were small, delicately shaped with very long fingernails that were polished bright red. They appeared flawless. The skin delicate and soft. Her oval-shaped nails were filed to perfection. And now they were groveling in this dirt next to Wynnie's own, seeking out clues to a past that was thousands upon thousands of years before their own time.

"Tell me, Wynnie, do you have any thoughts about continuing your education?"

"Continuing? I'm not sure what you mean."

"Well, you went to high school, didn't you?"

"I had to drop out when my father died. So, I never graduated."

"But I understand that you help out at the trading post. You help Lucille Samuels with the accounts and ordering."

"You don't need a high school diploma to do that." Wynnie laughed.

"But you could go to correspondence school. You know,

where they send the lessons in the mail to you. If you would get a high school diploma, you could then go on and get a degree in, say . . . accounting."

"I already do the accounts as you said. Not sure I really need a degree to do it."

"Oh, well, perhaps something else, like art history. Art history is fascinating, and you could go on and develop a special focus in the art of the southwest."

"But I live in the southwest and my grandmother was a rug weaver, one of the best."

"So, you know all about Navajo rugs, pottery, art of the Indians." Regina laughed softly.

"I know about it, and I know I myself am not at all artistic."

"Then what are you good at?"

"Fishing," Wynnie answered succinctly.

"Fishing, that's all? I . . . I mean . . . I don't mean 'that's all'. But where in heaven's name do you fish around here? I've barely seen a speck of water."

"I don't fish here. I go up north, by the Colorado border. And I do make awfully good fishing flies."

"Fishing flies. My late husband loved fly fishing."

"I tie the best wet flies around. Lucille carries them in her store. Last year I made almost six hundred dollars from my wet flies and another one hundred from the dry flies." She paused and took a strand of her own hair. "See that?"

"Yes, lovely glossy hair you have."

"Yep, the trout think so too. I can disguise a hook shank with that and make a stonefly body that can fool any trout in any season. Of course, you have to know the season stoneflies are hatching—the nymphs."

"But fly tying and fly fishing can't take you through life."

"Why not? I could become a guide. Rich people come out and they want a good guide."

"B–b–but . . . a girl guide? Do you think they'll want a girl guide?"

"If they can catch fish with a woman guide, why not?"

"Well, maybe," Regina said softly.

"Hey, what do you have there?" Wynnie said suddenly and

bent over to paw the bottom of the screen where Regina was working. It was another fragment similar to the petrified wood Wynnie found earlier. That had been Juniper wood, she had sworn.

"What is it?" Regina whispered.

"I found something like it a few minutes ago. It looks like . . ." Her voice dropped off.

"Like what?"

"It could be part of the same thing. But not sure what." Wynnie bent down and reached into a dish where she kept the small fragments from the screen. "Look, it could fit with this one." She held up the small piece of wood that appeared to match the one they had just found.

Wynnie looked up toward the cliffs to the west, the Canyon Ridge cliffs. She thought of when her Ami Sani had died. It was the first funeral she had gone to. She remembered crying the whole way on the steep ridge path to the trees where they would hoist Ami Sani's body to be safe from the vultures and to also keep the chindi, the ghosts, from following them, or the skinwalkers. Wynnie had grown very still, recalling that day. It was still in the deep shadows of the early morning when they had begun walking. There were clusters of juniper trees that grew straight up from the rock. Junipers were gravity-defying trees, and perhaps that was why they grew where the dead were taken on boards. To be placed in these trees was safe, as ground animals could not disturb them. The bodies were bound in wrapping that was so tough and tight on the boards that even the vultures gave up. And no chindi or ghosts would follow them then. A shiver ran down her spine. What could be the link between those juniper cliffs and the artifacts they were finding here, thousands of feet away?

This had not ever been a burial ground—too easy for the chindi to come, for the dead to go back to the home they came from. The last thing a family wanted was for their dead ancestors to visit them. That was why they were taken to the cliffs and put high in the trees that grew there. It would be too hard for the ghosts, the evil spirits, to follow them.

Wynnie felt Regina studying her carefully. She heard her take a deep breath. “Wynnie, may I ask you something?” Her entire tone had changed.

“Sure, Mrs. Phelps. I mean Regina.”

“You seemed uncomfortable last night when Gideon and Professor Acheson were praising you so lavishly for your find.” Wynnie felt a tremor run down her spine. “Was there any reason?”

“I . . . I . . . I’m not sure, Mrs. Phelps. I mean Regina.” She took a deep breath. “I’m not sure how I can explain this.”

“Try, Wynnie. Please try, because I’d like to know if we are somehow offending you by digging into your people’s past.” She paused and took a breath. “Well, I know there are rules about this. But I am sure Professor Acheson is very aware of them and is very sensitive to them.”

“Yes,” Wynnie replied softly.

“We are here as guests, really, on what is your land. This is Navajo reservation land. I think Acheson is especially careful to obtain the proper permits to dig here.”

“Yes,” Wynnie replied softly again.

“He knows the rules.”

“Of course.” Wynnie nodded.

The two words were not meant to be patronizing, but in that moment Regina realized that there was a gulf between her and Wynnie, and Wynnie’s people, that was not simply immense but uncrossable.

That night Regina could not sleep. She sensed that something was disturbing Wynnie deeply. She knew that the Indians were very superstitious people, but wasn’t it somewhat denigrating for white people to think that way about other cultures, other people? When she finally fell asleep, she had a disturbing dream. She had been walking in the desert across a wide patch of what some called desert silt, a very fine, floury type of sand. She was looking down at her feet and watching the impression they left when suddenly the footprints changed. They were not of her shoes but paws—a coyote’s paws. She dropped to the sand on her knees. Her hands too had dissolved and were now paws—a coyote’s paws. She shrieked into the night and sat up straight in her tent. It was very cold, and she wrapped her arms around her shoulders to keep from shivering. But were they hands? Or paws? Was she a skinwalker, as the people here called ghosts? Tears began to roll down Regina's face. She lay back down and, clamping her hands together, she saw the bright-red nail polish that her manicurist had so expertly painted on her nails a week before.

"Yes", she whispered into the night. Apple of my Eye. That was the name of the polish. I'm not a skinwalker. I am a human being, and my own manicurist paints my nails in this newest red color by the wonderful cosmetic firm Revlon. She had even met one of the handsome Revson brothers—was it Charles or Joseph? She had heard that one of them had a wandering eye and it had wandered right over to her at some gala in New York.

"I'm not a skinwalker," she whispered into the night. Who was she trying to convince? *What am I really . . . really, beyond being a very rich lady . . . who seeks . . . seeks what? Affirmation? Affirmation of what?*

She began to think about Douglas Acheson. She had committed a huge amount of money to this endeavor. She trusted him, he was after all a distinguished professor at Yale. His wife had died, and he was left feeling totally bereft. That was when he devoted himself entirely—heart, soul and mind, he had said—to this dig.

Regina, herself born into a humble family, had simply sought security, or so she thought. But when had security turned into something beyond money, something else entirely? She had begun craving something more; security was boring. Some sort of recognition beyond the things she could own or buy. What was it that Douglas Acheson had said to her after Wynnie had discovered that first artifact from goodness knows how many hundred—no, thousands of years before? "This will make me! You see, Regina, what an investment you made with me." "Investment." The word now shocked her. It was so crass.

Yes, she thought, *and what an investment I made when I married the King of Tires, Edward Phelps, who cheated on me on our honeymoon, no less? I am nothing. No, I am worse than nothing. I am a parasite. I own everything but in truth nothing. The whole world must be laughing at me, and especially the world out here.*

SEVEN

For five days straight, Georgia rode deep into the Bisti Badlands, reveling in the blackness of the terrain. It seemed like every day she found something new to paint. There were endless narratives of light and shadow, of texture and form on this land that on a certain level seemed so unvarying. On the fifth day, she and Orville got up hours before dawn and in the coolness of those hours rode their horses into town for more supplies. She wanted to first check and see if there was any news of Juan.

The whole way she was hoping against hope that the old man had returned. They had been friends for several years now, and he seemed to have an instinct for the kinds of bones she was drawn to. It was rather uncanny. She recalled how, on her last visit to the Black Place, he had insisted that she close her eyes while he gently took her hand and led her up to a spectacular set of antlers with perhaps a dozen points that spread at least four feet across. He knew her eye so well, and he appeared to get as much delight in finding these treasures as she did in painting them. The particular set he had found for her that time was truly spectacular and she knew she had to have it, and not simply to paint it. She wanted to hang it somewhere in her house. When she first glimpsed the antlers, she turned to Juan and said, "Isn't it interesting, Juan, that they are more alive to me than the actual animals walking around out here, their tails swishing, their eyes searching for their next place to graze or—" She glanced at a nearby coyote. "Or what to kill."

"You're an artist, Miss O'Keeffe. That's what artists are supposed to do. See what others don't see."

"But you see it too, Juan."

"But not like an artist." He laughed softly. "I'm more of a finder for an artist."

See what others don't see. The words lingered in her head. So why could she not see where Juan Nez was?

The old man had an almost courtly way about him. Often if they were walking together and the terrain became rough or a bit steep, he would take her elbow gently with one hand and walk or guide her up the hill. Juan, who was at least twenty years older, would guide her. He was so caring and so tender. She knew very little about his history or his family. He once mentioned that he had walked from Mexico to Far Cry here in New Mexico. She knew he had herded sheep and gone on cattle drives. On occasion a few bits would slip out. For one, he could cobble shoes. This surprised her.

"You don't say, you're a cobbler!"

"I do say, Miss O'Keeffe."

"What led you to do that?"

"Well, I fell in love with a girl's feet."

"What!" Georgia exclaimed. "You fell in love with her feet?"

"And the rest of her too." He gave a sly wink.

Georgia howled when he told her this.

"You taught yourself to make shoes for love."

"Sí."

"But how?"

"I think I just understood feet after walking from Mexico. I just had a sense of how a shoe should work."

"What happened to the girl?"

He sighed. "She walked away with another man."

"In the shoes you had made for her?"

"Sí, she loved those shoes."

"Oh no! That's so sad."

"Ah no, not that sad." He sighed again. "I wouldn't make that good of a husband."

"I don't believe that's true, Juan. I think you'd make a mighty fine husband."

He shrugged at that point. "Believe what you want, Miss O'Keeffe."

Georgia now realized that those were the last words he had ever spoken to her. Juan never said "hello" or "goodbye", for that matter. No "hasta la vista" or "adiós, mi amiga". It was usually twilight when they parted ways. The last time she saw him they had just returned from one of their walks in the Black Place. He had turned with his burro Pedro on the lead and simply walked away, melting into the dusk.

Now Georgia walked through the door of the trading post. Lucille was sitting behind the counter smoking a cigarette.

"Hello, Georgia," she greeted her.

"Hi Lucille," Georgia sighed. "Hate to ask, but any sign of Juan?"

Lucille shook her head wearily. She sighed too. "And I hate to say it, but I think . . . I think . . ."

"Oh, don't say it, Lucille!"

She felt tears about to start leaking from her eyes. *Don't you dare cry, Georgia Totto O'Keeffe.*

It was late afternoon when they rode back to their campsite from Far Cry. The one thing that Georgia liked about the desert, and particularly the Black Place, was its silence. The silence wrapped her in a cocoon with her thoughts of Juan, to try and make sense of the nonsensical. And Juan's disappearance was senseless. In silence things flourished, blossomed. Silence was magical. It could coax images, thoughts, colors out of barrenness. It was one of the things that Georgia loved most about Ryan—his silence. But this silence offered none of those blessings. This silence was alien.

As they rode back, Orville had suggested a new route that he felt Georgia would find interesting. The grays and the ashen tones near the eroded hills were now cast in a reddish hue. The gulches and canyons narrowed. "We're coming into the region of the slot canyons," Orville announced.

"Slot canyon. Never heard the term. Something rare, I guess."

"Around here, yes, but not in Utah. There must be hundreds of them in Utah."

"Why the word 'slot'?"

"That's just what they are—very narrow canyons. Just slivers in the rocks compared to most canyons. Sometimes not wide enough for people to walk side by side. But you're going to love them. I'll take you to one that's on our way home."

Twenty minutes later they dismounted their horses and walked down an embankment.

"OK, suck in your guts, Georgia." Orville pointed to a crack in the sedimentary rock ahead.

She followed him into an opening that was no more than twenty inches wide. She had to turn sideways to walk and, even then, her nose often scraped the side walls. Lucky she wasn't claustrophobic, she thought.

"You with me?" he called as she inched her way along behind him.

"I better not gain any weight, or I won't make it," she replied.

"It widens ahead in another fifty feet or so."

"OK. What if I see a rattlesnake? I didn't bring my snake stick with me."

"Pray."

But another twenty feet into the slot, she wasn't thinking about rattlesnakes or praying anymore. She looked up from this slot in these ancient sediments and saw a piece of the sky. Just a piece. A piece of heaven that felt as if Orville had plucked it out from the rest of the sky just for her. She gasped.

"You OK, Georgia?"

"Oh my God, Orville this is the most beautiful thing I have ever seen." The sky unfurled overhead like a ribbon. She had to come back in full light and not twilight as it was now. She wanted to see it blue and rippling like a flag overhead. She felt as though she had just found a secret treasure, a jewel that would burn in her imagination until she had painted it, not just once but a thousand times.

"I've got to come back here," she murmured. "Come back in full light." She tipped her head up.

"Full light," Orville repeated. He was several yards in front of her.

"How did you hear that?" Georgia asked. "I was just whispering to myself."

"Odd sound effects here because of the shape of the slot. You'd have to ask a scientist, but sound waves carry."

Her sister Anita just last year had traveled to London and told her about visiting St. Paul's Cathedral and the Whispering

Gallery. Anita had described how the sound carried in a wave from one corner of the vast cathedral to another. She had written a long letter to Georgia describing the "miracle" of this cathedral. The whispers cling to the walls, apparently, and travel around. "Robert and I tried it. Great fun. He recited to me a slightly naughty limerick and I heard every word."

Well, Georgia thought, looking at the red rock walls of the slot, *this is my kind of cathedral*.

"Hey, Orville, how about I whisper a limerick to you? See if you get it."

"OK, try me."

"Gotta think for a minute. Only naughty limericks come to mind."

"Best kind," Orville replied.

She suddenly recalled one she had heard in a favorite bar of hers and Stieglitz in New York. "OK, here I go."

> "Recently, a man called
> Martin
> told his ex-wife:
> Since we've been partin'
> I've had women and men
> Several geese and a hen
> and a Hoover,
> and that's just for startin'."

"Georgia O'Keeffe, shame on you!" Orville did not whisper but roared. "A Hoover vacuum cleaner! Jesus Christ, Georgia!"

"Careful there, Orville, you might cause an earthquake or something."

It was almost dark as they came out of the slot. They walked back to where they had tied up their horses and remounted. They had not gone far. Georgia was in the lead. The moon was just rising, full and luminous like an immense silver bubble trembling on the black hills. To the right the first stars of Orion's Belt were rising. She felt a shiver that made the hairs on the back of her neck stand up straight. There was a presence here. She felt the muscles on Dottie's back contract as well. Did the horse feel it too? She kept her eyes straight ahead.

Then in the moonlight she saw something that caught her breath. It was whiter than the moon. The immense branching antlers of a mule deer rose majestically against the sky. They seemed suspended in the twilight near the two brightest stars of the constellation, Rigel and Betelgeuse. "Just for you, Georgia." The words of Juan Nez echoed in her ears. Those were the four words with which he would always greet her when he presented her with a skull or pelvis. The antlers seemed like a distant echo in her mind. His toothless grin would crease his face. "Thought you would like this, dearie." He always called her "dearie" when he had a special find for her. And there it was waiting for her—the stars suspended within the tangle of antlers.

"Juan," she whispered. "Juan?" She could almost feel his hand on her elbow, guiding her toward the antlers.

EIGHT

Georgia left the antlers just where they were. Normally she would have taken them back with her to paint another day. But they seemed to belong where she had found them. "I'll leave it for now." She whispered the words into the night. She knew that Juan had been there. She was certain. It was as if his spirit still lingered. It would be wrong to remove them, at least not now. She would come back tomorrow and paint them exactly where the antlers were, which was close to the entrance of the slot canyon. She didn't want to disturb this place in the least. She must come back and paint and think and see.

There was a lot waiting for her there near the slot canyon and in it. The unfurling blue flag of sky revealed by the breach in the rock. The strangeness of that deep fissure she had walked through, the whispers beneath the silence. The invisible wind that stirred the fine hairs on the back of her neck as she had ridden toward the antlers. No, things must be left in place and if she were patient enough, and quiet enough, who knew what else might be revealed?

The next day at the crack of dawn Georgia went to paint the antlers. When the dawn light was gone, and the day grew hotter, she retreated to the slot canyon to watch the sky move through its endlessly shifting iterations through that breach in the rock. There was no room in the narrowness of the slot for her painting gear and easel, but that didn't matter. The absence of her tools made her eyes keener. On the sixth day she returned from the slot canyon just as Gideon Blake was riding up to their camp.

"Hey all!" he cried out. "We made another astonishing discovery today and would like to invite y'all for the celebration, courtesy of Regina Phelps. More champagne and, yes, if you like fish eggs, we'll even have caviar. Never tasted it myself. And prime steaks brought in from Houston."

"Well, what is the discovery?" David McAlpin asked.

"All I can tell you is that it's another pre-Clovis artifact. Seeing will be believing."

It had been a long day for Georgia and the last thing she needed was champagne and caviar. How ridiculous! People were hungry out here. The Navajos in this region were amongst the poorest. It was hard to raise sheep here; farming was next to impossible. Drugs and alcohol riddled the region. But Orville urged her to go, promising to ride back with her if she wanted to leave early.

When she arrived half an hour later with Orville, McAlpin and Ansel, the party was in full swing. She was pleased to see Wynnie Haloke presiding over the grill.

"Look at you," she said.

"Yep," Wynnie replied. "Mrs. Phelps is sending three steaks home with me for my family."

At just that moment Regina Phelps floated up to the grill in a ridiculous chiffon gown. She was also wearing a stunning Kenneth Begay turquoise necklace. Begay was one of the foremost living Navajo jewelers.

"That's a Kenneth Begay necklace, isn't it?" Georgia asked.

"It is, Miss O'Keeffe."

"Just call me Georgia, please. I think I saw his exhibit at the Metropolitan Museum in New York four or five years ago. It certainly becomes you."

"Why thank you. I know, it's ridiculous—me all gussied up. But it's such an extraordinary find they made today, and I think you, Wynnie, were the one to unearth it again."

"Me and Mr. Blake together."

"All of you, Wynnie in quadrant four." Blake now walked up and gave her a pat on the back. "She got down to—what was it—the fifth stratum, we had just opened it up and she was scraping away and out popped a pottery sherd that was quite unusual. Take Miss O'Keeffe and her friends over to our display table and show them. Someone else can cover the grill for you."

"OK," Wynnie said softly and led Georgia and the others over to the table where they displayed the latest finds.

"There it is." Wynnie pointed.

Blake soon came over as well. "Again, we feel it predates the Anasazi era by thousands of years. But on this, you see the suggestion of a crude design that eventually became what some call the Sacred Rainbow of the Anasazi." Georgia was not looking just at the pottery fragment, but Wynnie, who seemed to flinch as Blake spoke the words "Sacred Rainbow" and picked up the piece. He held it out toward Wynnie, who appeared to recoil slightly. "Your find, Wynnie. You hold it."

"No, sir, I don't want to break it."

"It's already broken, Wynnie." He laughed, then turned to Georgia. "She's much too shy. Doesn't want to take any credit for it."

Georgia looked at Wynnie. *She doesn't want to even touch that piece*, Georgia thought. He might as well be asking her to pet a rattlesnake. She seemed as if she had somehow removed herself from the scene. Her eyes avoided even looking at the piece.

Georgia also noticed that Regina was standing back and regarding Wynnie with what she would almost call motherly concern. It surprised Georgia. Was Regina familiar with the Navajo superstitions? Ryan had told Georgia about some. There was one that had to do with rainbows. She had been hiking with Ryan once and a rainbow appeared over a mesa. She pointed to it, and he grabbed her hand. "You know, my dear, there's an old saying that if you point at a rainbow with your finger, the rainbow will cut it off. And then you couldn't paint anymore."

"Oh yes, I could. The rainbow would have to cut them all off and then I'd just paint with the brush between my teeth."

Ryan laughed. "I bet you would, Georgia. I bet you would."

Georgia walked a few feet over toward Regina. "Quite a find, isn't it?" she said in a low voice.

"It really is, I suppose," Regina answered.

"What do you mean 'suppose'?" Georgia asked.

"Well, you know she—I mean Wynnie—seems slightly

unsettled by it. Do you suppose she regrets somehow digging into the past, disturbing it in some way?" Regina's words caught Georgia by surprise. She would never have expected this reaction. "I mean I am so glad we can help these people." By "these people", Georgia realized she meant the Navajos. "I would like to help Wynnie in particular. You know she shows a lot of potential."

"In what way could you help her?"

"Perhaps money to continue her education, or something. I do want to talk to her about it more. Yet I don't want to be intrusive."

"I don't think it would be."

"I'm first going to talk to a friend of mine at Yale, Sam Wolfe, to inquire about perhaps establishing a scholarship or a fund of some sort, where the money could go to these Indian people who help us so much on various digs."

"That would be good," Georgia said. "We take their help for granted. And pay them very little, I would expect."

It was growing late. The last of the moon had dipped beneath the horizon. And the stars had begun to follow. Within minutes it would be the pitch of the night without a squeak of light. It was almost as if Georgia could feel her irises expanding in hopes that the pupil of her eye could capture any random light. She was tempted to scold that silly iris. She wanted to say: *Be pleased with the light you have already gathered today. Don't become a glutton for light. Revel now in the pitch blackness of this night and you will see all the better tomorrow, and love the light even more.*

Georgia mounted her pinto and with her friends rode back in silence to their camp. She was thinking how easy it was to misjudge a person. She had certainly misjudged Regina Phelps. Who would have thought she cared a bit about Wynnie?

"So, what do you think?" Ansel said.

"About what?" McAlpin asked.

"About the latest find—the rainbow arc thing."

"Well," McAlpin began. "That find today, in addition to the previous one, most likely means that this dig will be underwritten for the next five years. A dream come true for any archaeologist."

"S'pose so," Orville replied. "At least the relic hunters won't get it."

"At least?" McAlpin said.

"They don't know what they're doing, the relic hunters. They can destroy a site for those people, real archaeologists who at least know how to excavate properly."

"But how many Indians are hired for these proper excavations? I swear Wynnie is the first one we've encountered," McAlpin asked.

"True," Orville said.

"And are they paying her anything?" Georgia replied. "Well, a couple of prime sirloin steaks for her family, and probably some lowly daily wage. The students on this dig get paid nothing, but they'll come out with college degrees and the possibility of leading their own digs sometime. Mrs. Phelps might give Wynnie tuition fees for a college education along with the steaks?"

"Ain't going to happen, Georgia," Orville replied.

"I assumed it. That's what angers me."

"Don't lose sleep on it, Georgia," Orville said as they dismounted and turned in for the night.

But she did lose a little sleep. What if Regina's good intentions weren't followed through? Why was she so blessed and Wynnie not? Why did Wynnie have white folks crawling all over her ancestral land, tossing her scraps of steak while they cashed in on their white privilege for grants, fellowships, and the beneficence of outrageously rich Americans who would get their name on buildings of fancy universities? There was already a building at Yale named after the Phelpses.

"Jesus Christ, life is unfair," Georgia muttered as she drifted off to sleep and finally found peace in that scrap of blue sky that floated over the gash in the rock of the slot canyon. How odd that the narrow gash seemed to reveal an entire universe to her.

NINE

Wynnie Haloke could not sleep that night. She had tried everything to avoid picking that pottery piece out of the screening box when she first spotted it. A dread had run through her. She had been tempted to throw it away, but it was at just the moment she discovered it that Blake had come by.

"Got anything interesting?" he had asked.

"Not really," she said.

"Don't be so sure. What's that?"

"What's what?" Wynnie had said.

"Wynnie, it's right in front of your eyes. I think it's something significant. Your screen, you dug it up, so you should do the honors."

Her hand had trembled as it hovered over the piece. She tried to banish what she was seeing. The arc unfolding like an unborn rainbow. It was sacred. No one should be touching this. No white person nor even an Indian woman. This was for shamans. And shamans alone.

Was this a kiva that the professor was excavating? Or had it been at one time? She lay awake and thought about the meaning of all this. There were rules about white people messing with kivas. And rules about women of any color entering some kivas. Had the professor reported this site to the tribal council? He must have known that he should if it was a kiva or even suspected to be one. How could he not? A kiva could run to great depths, as deep as thirty feet or forty. But things were known to rise to the top or higher if there were minor earthquakes. Of course, one fragment of rock or wood with a sacred design did not make a kiva. But still she was uncomfortable. Something just didn't seem right. She was no archaeologist, but the more she thought about it, the more peculiar it seemed.

Was the geological strata really that old here, she wondered. There were other places that might be older. But there was no absolute method of dating an artifact, at least not yet. However, Wynnie had heard some of the students talking about new ways for dating that were being developed. Something with carbon. She had tried to ask one student, but he had said, "It's really complicated to explain. I'm not sure you'd understand." Then he gave her a quick smile as if to say: "Not to be insulting." But of course, it was insulting. She wondered if someday she'd get up her nerve to say something back. Something mild like: "Well, try me."

But whatever this new method might be, the carbon thing, as of now it was all dependent on examining the minerals above and below the sedimentary rock. In short, it was all relative but there could be no absolute proof of age. However, for her to be touching a sacred object from an Anasazi kiva was not good. How would she explain this to Blake, who had been hanging over her at the time of her discovery, let alone Professor Acheson? She had been lucky to be hired. Who was she to tell them that she had doubts? Would they understand that for those who touched these sacred things they could be cursed, unless a shaman was there to dispel the curse? She tried to imagine herself walking up to Professor Acheson and suggesting that they should perhaps bring a shaman to the dig site to dispel any curse. She almost laughed out loud at her own naivete.

But now she wondered if she should at least tell Tommy Tso. She had accused him of flirting with Mrs. Phelps when she had first arrived and was in the trading post. He had laughingly dismissed her concerns.

"Come on, Wynnie. I'm just joking with her. Part of the tourist business. These white ladies come out here with their notions of the wild west, cowboys and Indians. They come with their movie dreams."

"But I'm not in a movie."

"You want to be in the movies?"

"No, I want to take them fishing. I'd get paid a lot for that."

"I could fix that up for you. I got a lot of real estate clients who like to fish."

Then they had made up. Make-up sex was always good. He explained that he just needed to stay on the good side of Mrs. Phelps.

"She has a good side?" Wynnie had laughed harshly.

"C'mon, Wynnie," Tommy said.

"Come on where?"

"She's twenty years older than me. I just really want her to buy that property over there west of Window Rock."

Nevertheless, Wynnie spent a sleepless night. The money that she was making on the dig was all right. The steaks were good . . . but white people, white people got on her nerves.

Now it was almost time to cook breakfast for the camp.

Georgia skipped breakfast that morning, even though Orville had made pancakes.

"Come on, Georgia. These are my special pancakes. You love them."

"I gotta get out there, Orville. All your fault. You showed me the slot canyon and then afterward the antlers. I tell you, I was overwhelmed. The land is incredible."

"Tell you what, I'll pack up a half dozen pancakes for you, and you can eat them with jam when you get out there to paint the darn antlers."

"Blessed antlers. The most beautiful I've ever seen." She did not mention Juan. However, there was this moment when she had stepped closer to look at those antlers, and she swore she felt his presence. It wasn't strange at all. It was oddly comforting. She imagined that toothless smile of his, the creased brown skin, his braided hair often flashing bright ribbons woven into the plaits . . .

The sun was still low on the horizon by the time Georgia saw the antlers again. "Perfect," she whispered, digging her heels into Dottie's flanks to urge her on. But Dottie suddenly seemed a tad skittish.

"What's ailing you, dear?" She looked up and saw a shred of something red blowing in the breeze. It had fetched up on one of the smaller branching antlers. Was this what had upset Dottie? Georgia dismounted, tied the horse to a large clump of sagebrush and walked off toward the antlers that were less than one hundred feet away.

The scarlet ribbon quivered in the breeze between the two tines that branched from one of the horns. Georgia freed it. She knew this must be from one of Juan's braids. *So, where are you, my friend?*

Suddenly a chilly breeze stirred the air. She tucked the ribbon in her pocket and looked at Dottie. The horse seemed to be happily munching on the sagebrush.

Georgia decided to set up her easel in this particular spot. But it was hard for her to concentrate. The very air of the place seemed affected by something unutterable, intangible. There were endless skinwalker stories that swirled across the Navajo reservation lands. Had she disturbed a skinwalker by trying to find Juan? Skinwalkers were those freakish, harmful spirits—witches that took animal forms and often were the first to be blamed in the deadliest of crimes. Ryan did not believe in them at all. But every year it seemed that someone was blaming a skinwalker for some crime or another.

"I think we're becoming more and more medieval," Ryan had said when someone blamed a gas station robbery on a coyote that had been lurking around the premises over in Agua Roja. It was said that if you shone a light on a skinwalker, their eyes glowed red. "But the same is true of rabbits," Ryan had pointed out in a court hearing. He'd even brought a rabbit into court, cuddling it in his arms as he stood in front of the judge. The entire courtroom burst into laughter. "The point is, your honor, did the plaintiff stand close enough to this 'coyote' to see that it was not a coyote at all, but possibly a rabbit?"

"Objection, your honor, it was not a rabbit," the lawyer interrupted. "It was a coyote that my client saw, and definitely not a rabbit."

"Maybe the rabbit had been apprehended by the coyote and was hanging from its mouth when the flashlight was on him, sir," Ryan replied.

"Enough of your antics, Sheriff McCaffrey," the judge scolded.

Ryan had related this story gleefully to Georgia. When Georgia had replied that he was lucky the judge hadn't kicked him out of the courtroom, Ryan protested. "Are you kidding? Judge Miller and I are best friends. We always go out for a beer after a case closes. You'd love Harry Miller."

"Why's that?"

"Why's that?" Ryan replied. "Well, for one, he's got a sense of humor. And he's sort of a . . . a . . . polymath."

"Polymath? Never heard you use that word."

"Well, I don't know many polymaths, in fact only one. Harry Miller."

"What sort of polys does he have—or do?"

"He's a doctor and he has a degree in astronomy and archaeology in addition to his law degree. And . . ."

"I'm waiting."

"He's a champion bowler."

"You had me at astronomy."

"A man of many talents."

Georgia now stared at the antlers and tried to imagine a rabbit putting the scarlet ribbon in the prongs. She set up her easel and got to work. She was uncertain how long it was before she made her first brushstroke, however she definitely felt a chill run down her spine. Within seconds she caught a bright twinkle between the antlers where the ribbon had snagged. The twinkle was Venus. It was rare for her to be able to catch that star in the morning, for it rose in the east just minutes into the dawn. It was there only briefly before the full morning light blotted out the nighttime constellations, and it was long after Coyote had shaken out the star blanket to cause the massive befuddlement of a starry night. Now there was just one star, shining brightly. A few tears began to leak from Georgia's eyes, blurring that morning star. *He's dead, I know it. He's dead. Juan is dead.*

"Adiós, Juan; adios, mi amigo," she whispered into the breaking light.

TEN

Wynnie had caught a ride into town with one of the Yale students. She would resupply the camp and spend the night in Far Cry, heading back the next day. She hoped to be spending the night at Tommy's place. In the meantime, she was helping Lucille stock the back room with newly arrived inventory.

"No news of Juan?" Wynnie asked Lucille.

"No, I think Pablo has almost given up."

"Poor kid." Wynnie sighed.

"How is it working out there on the dig?"

Wynnie waited a minute. She wasn't sure how to answer the question because in fact she was seriously considering quitting the dig. But she wouldn't know how to explain it to Lucille, or to any white person for that matter.

"OK, I guess."

"You guess?"

"The pay is all right."

"Yes, I imagine so. I can't match Yale University for paying what they do."

Wynnie chuckled. "Is it Yale or is it Mrs. Regina Phelps?"

"Good question," Lucille said. "She's a looker for her age."

"I guess so," Wynnie replied glumly.

"Now, don't get your panties in a twist." Panties in a twist, Lucille had the oddest sayings. "She's just flirting with Tommy and I bet you she's at least twenty years older than he is."

"Who says I'm interested in Tommy?"

"Not me!" Lucille almost barked. "Speaking of the devil . . ."

At just that moment Tommy Tso walked in.

"What are you doing here, Wynnie? Don't tell me you got fired."

"No! I'm here picking up supplies and going out again tomorrow at the crack of dawn."

He slid up to her while Lucille's back was turned and whispered. "I hope not the crack." A wave of relief washed through Wynnie. *He loves me . . . Bet that old lady has a wrinkly butt and floppy old boobs.*

Four hours later they were in bed together at Tommy's house.

Ever since Wynnie had found the first potsherd, she had worried as to whether she should tell Tommy about it. His uncle was a shaman and would know the significance of the rainbow symbol, if indeed that's what it was.

After another session of lovemaking, Wynnie stayed on top of him and said, "I got to talk to you about something."

"Oh really!" he said, smiling softly as he reached up and twined some of her long hair through his fingers. "Don't ever cut your hair, by the way."

"That's what I believe they call a non sequitur if there ever was one." She slapped him playfully. "I bet you didn't think I knew those fancy words. Well, I do. It means something that doesn't follow."

"Like sex."

"Oh, be quiet."

"So, what do you want to tell me? What is this thing that doesn't follow making love to you?"

"I don't really know. I think I'm just finding it weird out there with the white folks digging into our history. They're getting paid for it. Like strangers coming into, say, my grandma's attic, but they're not part of the family. And if they do discover something fantastic—what do they do? Haul it off to some white man's museum?

"There are starting to be rules about digging on sacred sites out here. Not enough. Still, there are rules. I've got to think about this some more." She paused and sighed. "Would you ever consider going and talking to your Uncle Edgar about this? About the new rules regarding sacred lands? I can even draw the latest potsherd that I found on a piece of paper for you. It has a rainbow arc on it, and I think it might be sacred."

"I have to think, Wynnie. I kind of doubt the land where they are digging is sacred. I mean, this professor guy should know. He's from Yale after all." He paused and looked deep into her dark eyes. "Maybe you should quit the dig."

"I was thinking about it, but I can't quit. My family needs the money. My grandmother needs an operation. My mom is sinking into one of her depressions and can't work at the gas station right now."

Tommy climbed out of bed. Her eyes followed him. He had the most beautiful ass in the world. An odd thought crossed her mind. Miss O'Keeffe should stop painting the mesas and hoodoos, and paint Tommy Tso's ass. Or maybe his dick when it was aroused—better than any hoodoo. She giggled to herself.

"What's so funny?" He turned around and smiled.

Oh dear, he was ready to go again. He leaped onto the bed.

"One more time," he whispered.

Sure, why not? she thought.

ELEVEN

In Richmond, Virginia, Marya Phelps Armstrong walked into the Hamilton, Martin and Perkins law office to see Bruce Hamilton.

"May I help you, Mam?" a secretary asked.

"I'm expected. I'm here to see Mr. Hamilton."

"You have an appointment?"

"I don't need an appointment," she paused. "You must be new."

"Yes, Mam, and whom should I say is calling?"

"Marya Phelps." She always dropped Armstrong. She had barely been married long enough to the jerk to warrant the embossed stationery, not to mention the Armstrong monogrammed silverware.

"Yes, right away, Mam." She picked up the phone. "Mr. Hamilton, Miss Marya Phelps is here to speak to you."

"Marya you say?" he growled. Then sighed. "Send her in."

Bruce Hamilton was well over six feet tall. He had played football at Yale, was on the board of trustees at Yale and the most prominent lawyer in Virginia. He was also a direct descendent of Thomas Jefferson, and some even say Sally Hemings, Jefferson's Black mistress and slave, was his three-times great-grandmother. But everyone agrees that Bruce Hamilton is the smartest lawyer below the Mason-Dixon Line.

He came out from behind the desk and shook her hand. He didn't need to ask what she was here for but, being a gentleman, he did.

"Now, what can I do for you, my dear? You're looking especially lovely this morning. Have you been out for a ride on that frisky gelding?"

She was dying to say that she had ridden a friskier mount, and it wasn't a gelding, but by God those Navajo could fuck. Had it only been last month?

"I want to know if you have checked on that one clause about the loan."

"I have. It's not going to work, Marya. Such a loan has very strict stipulations."

"But you know the settlement isn't fair."

"I don't know that. I am not hired to be a judge about fairness. And honestly, fairness doesn't hold up in court in matters like these. By any standards your father was quite generous."

"But the point is he was more generous to Regina and I'm his own flesh and blood. He left all that money to digging up dead civilizations and stupid artifacts."

"But one of the Georgia O'Keeffe pictures he's left to you."

"I don't give a fuck abut Georgia O'Keeffe. I think she's a lousy painter," she snapped then settled back in her chair.

"What happens to the money when Regina dies? The real estate?"

"A large portion goes to Yale, of course, and they will decide how the archaeology department can best use it. That will be decided by Professor Acheson, I suppose, if he is still at Yale. Which I'm sure he will be, as he is up for the Phelps chair of archaeology."

"But I am still having to live in her house, Bridlemere, but don't own it."

"You don't have to live there. You have a very luxurious apartment in Leesville and an apartment in Palm Beach, Florida."

"But I want a house where I can keep my horses to myself."

"Regina has been very generous about allowing you to keep your horses at Bridlemere and she even takes care of the vet bills, as I understand."

"But it's not my house. I want a house of my own."

"She called me recently and said she would like to give you one of *her* Georgia O'Keeffe paintings."

"Which one? The Jack-in-the-Pulpit?"

"She didn't specify, but I doubt it would be that one as she is particularly fond of it."

"Ha! Have you seen that pulpit painting?"

"Yes, just after it arrived."

"Well, I think it looks like a penis with a hood on it. Disgusting."

"Disgusting? How disgusting is twenty-five thousand dollars?"

"That's worth twenty-five thousand dollars?"

"Yes, it is. It was just evaluated. We're not out of the depression yet. Farms in Loudoun County aren't worth as much. You can buy a Derby winner for that, these days. The last Derby winner sold for less than twenty-three thousand dollars, lowest price in years, but you have to feed and care for it. The O'Keeffe painting will skyrocket when the depression is over. Right now it's the highest price ever paid for an American painting.

"But paintings aside, let me clarify how this inheritance is structured. Upon Regina's passing, you will inherit all her assets since she has no children.

"Hmmm . . ." Marya said. She appeared somewhat placated, but nevertheless she wondered how long she would have to wait. Regina wasn't old, maybe fifty or fifty-five.

"Could I somehow borrow against it?"

"You'd have to work that out with Regina. She might be amenable. It would save her a lot in taxes." He paused. "But as I said you'd have to work it out with her."

"Yes, yes, of course."

TWELVE

Georgia had not told Orville about the ribbon she had found that was just like the ones Juan wove into his braids. She wasn't sure why not. It had seemed to her like a message of some sort, a private message and not to be shared. But what if it was not a message but rather a clue? Then she might be accused of withholding evidence. But right now, something was holding her back. She wasn't sure what. Maybe she didn't belong here at all. Many of the regions near the Black Place were called sacred lands. This could be part of those lands for all she knew. God knew the light was sacred in her eyes.

Nevertheless, she went back to paint the antlers in the early light and then she would retreat to the slot canyon, which she continued to explore and find new apertures to see the sky. The path in the slot canyon seemed to wander endlessly like a rock maze. She was careful to note where she had started so she could find her way back. At one point she thought she heard the trickle of water. But it was hard to tell where it was coming from, given the sound distortions of the tunnel. At another place she thought she heard the sound of breathing, but then she realized that in some inscrutable way the slot canyon had captured the whispers of the wind. She had tipped her head back for an instant and then stopped short, for above her a herd of small white clouds stampeded across the blue sky. This particular image would lurk in her mind's eye for another thirty years before she painted the scene that she had captured when she had tipped up her head. *I'll need a huge canvas for that,* she thought, and walked on.

On this same day, after Wynnie Haloke had left to go back to the dig, Tommy Tso drove up to the hogan of his Uncle Edgar, who lived out on the old Frontera road. He saw his Aunt Alice tending the chickens in a coyote-proof enclosure.

"Hi Auntie," Tommy called out. She went on spreading some chicken feed and must not have heard him.

Finally, she looked up and caught sight of him. "Yá'át'ééh," she called.

"Yá'át'ééh," he answered. She stepped toward the wire fencing of the enclosure.

"Is Uncle Edgar about? Does he have time for a talk?"

"Why you only speak hello in Navajo—those fancy boots suck all the Navajo out of you?"

"Hope not," he said, laughing.

"How much those boots cost you, Nephew?"

"Enough." He laughed. "How is Uncle?"

She looked toward the outhouse. "He's moving his bowels."

Oh, thank you for that information, Auntie, Tommy thought. "Uh . . . I'll wait."

"Good idea," she said, turning back to the chickens.

The door to the outhouse opened and his uncle came out. His long braids almost reached his knees. All Tommy could think was that he hoped his uncle kept the braids out of the toilet. God, how he had hated living here. He was sent to his aunt and uncle when his own father had got locked up in jail for drunkenness after his mom died. The choice had been to stay here or be sent to one of the Indian boarding schools.

"Yá'át'ééh, Shizhé'é Yázhí." Tommy strode forward.

"So, what brings you here, Nephew? Real estate business falling off?"

"Not yet. We're just getting started."

"Yes, I worry about that."

"Not to worry, Uncle. The more white people we get out here, the more work for us folks. Economy improves."

"Yeah, and the old ways die. You wait and see."

"Old ways don't need to die."

"Wait and see," his uncle growled. "Wóshdę́ę́', wóshdę́ę́'." He motioned for him to come along. Tommy followed his uncle into the hogan, which was twenty yards or so away. They entered the eight-walled structure through the eastern-facing door as was traditional with all hogans. It being midday, the sun poured in through that only door casting a luminous reddish light over everything. All the logs forming the eight walls seemed to glow from the reflected sunlight and the exposed timber of the hogan. In the center was a wood-burning stove with its chimney climbing straight up through a hole in the ceiling. On a western wall was a bed. On the southern wall there had been another bed for when Tommy lived there, but that had now been turned into a visitors' couch. There was a bureau as well, and a large table.

"So, what brings you here? You need healing? I just did a sand painting ceremony for Lester Etsitty from over in Window Rock. He had problems . . . you know, in his . . ." Edgar pointed to his crotch.

"No, Uncle, nothing like that. No healing required, at least not yet."

A wide smile burst across Uncle Edgar's face. "Not yet. Not yet you say. But just you wait . . . then the girls will have to wait."

Oh God, Tommy thought. If he got started, this could go on into a history of how much impotency Uncle Edgar had cured, then urinary issues, gnats in the aziz. A skinwalker who specialized in giving men prostate problems.

"Look, Uncle Edgar, I know you're the best shaman around and no one can make the sand paintings like you do for curing anything."

"Yeah, I had a kid here the other day, and they were going to rip out part of her throat—a tonsillectomy, they called it. They came to me but I—"

Tommy cut him off, "Yeah, yeah you told me about that before, but this has nothing to do with any body parts."

"Oh!" his uncle said softly. Tommy felt as if he had disappointed the old man.

"Look, I have to show you something." He reached into his pocket and took out the pencil drawing of the rainbow arc fragment that Wynnie had drawn for him.

Uncle Edgar took it and looked it over several times, then reached into his pocket for a broken set of spectacles.

"This is sacred." Uncle Edgar sighed, looking up. The fracture in the one lens of the spectacles appeared to distort his eye so that the iris of that eye seemed fractured as well. "Where did she find this?"

It took fifteen minutes for Tommy to explain to his uncle about the archaeology dig, the sifting screens, the purported age, and how this was all determined by stratigraphy.

Occasionally, his uncle would mutter the word diyin, meaning "sacred" in Navajo.

The paper with the picture trembled in his hands and then, after another several minutes, he began to speak in English, and it seemed as if his voice smoldered. "There is no way this could be found—not with the other . . . what did you call them . . .?"

"Artifacts."

"Yes, artifacts from a kiva. A very, very old kiva, maybe even a house from before there were kivas." He inhaled. "A . . . a pit house, perhaps."

His uncle began to shake uncontrollably. His face turned gray.

"Uncle . . . Uncle, are you . . ."

Uncle Edgar slumped over.

THIRTEEN

"You see, David, I 'make' a picture to give you the equivalent of what I felt. Nature is a vast chaotic collection of shapes. I try to create configurations out of chaos." Ansel and McAlpin were hunched over some prints he had just brought out from his portable darkroom. "See this. Those are rocks, near the ledges just west of here—the erosion makes them seem to almost move, to animate them until they look like rivers washing against the sky."

"This new color film," McAlpin asked. "What do you make of it?"

"I can get a far greater sense of color through a well-planned black and white image than I have ever achieved with color photography."

"And what about you, Georgia?" McAlpin turned to her.

"What about me?"

"What do you think about color as opposed to black and white?"

"I do both. I was mad for charcoal twenty years ago or so. I found that there was a certain movement I could capture with charcoal. I'm not sure what exactly I was thinking at the time, or why I decided to limit myself to it. It might have been that I felt the need for some sort of psychological cleansing exercise.

"I began with charcoal and paper and decided not to use any color until it was impossible to do what I wanted to do in black and white. I remember I began in March, and I believe it was June before I needed blue."

"*Needed* blue." McAlpin laughed softly.

"*Craved* blue was more like it. It was hunger."

Georgia thought to herself how she had rediscovered blue in the last few days in the slot canyon. Once again, she couldn't get enough of it. Perhaps it was from all the days in the Black

Place—sifting the blacks, the grays, into a spectrum of shadows had in some way unleashed this lust for blue again.

"Craving blue . . . I like that," McAlpin almost whispered. "I really like that. Maybe we could put on an exhibition at Princeton called 'Craving Blue'."

Georgia laughed. "Well, I can take you and show what has been satiating my appetite for blue lately, if you can part from Ansel."

"It's a deal!" McAlpin said.

Tommy Tso and his Aunt Alice were finally allowed in to see his uncle in the intensive care room at the Farmington hospital. Auntie Alice was hanging onto her nephew's arm. She began speaking in a fast, soft flow of Navajo.

Tommy looked down at his uncle. It seemed as if there were tubes coming out of all parts of him. It was when the nurse came up to adjust one that he noticed the tattoo on Uncle Edgar's chest.

"What's that?" he gasped.

"What's what?" the nurse asked. It was the same figure that Wynnie had drawn on the paper that was still tucked in his pants pocket.

"A tattoo, I guess," Tommy replied.

A gurgling sound came from his uncle's throat and he tried to motion Tommy with his hand. Tommy leaned over.

"What is it, Uncle?"

"Tell Hosteen Tsinajine . . ."

"Tell him what?"

His uncle raised a trembling finger to his chest and pointed at the tattoo.

The nurse now moved in with a stethoscope.

"He's going," she whispered and looked up with sympathetic eyes toward Tommy and his aunt.

Going? Tommy thought. *Going where?*

A terrible, wild cry reverberated through the room as Auntie Alice collapsed on the floor. The nurse wheeled around.

"Mam! Mam!" She bent down on her knees, then looked

up while she pressed the stethoscope to the old woman's chest.

"I can't believe this!" The nurse looked up. Her face was pale. "Both!"

"Both what?" Tommy asked.

"Dead. Both dead." She looked at her wristwatch. "At two minutes after three o'clock."

Two hours later, after signing the hospital paperwork, Tommy climbed back in his car and drove out on the old Valdez road. He was quite honestly in some sort of shock himself. He felt as if he had violated sacred lands.

He pulled to the side of the road and gripped the steering wheel. A cold sweat broke out on his forehead and he tried to calm his breathing. But his heart was racing. Why had he ever shown his uncle that drawing? Is that what had caused him to die? After all they had given him when his own mother and father had died . . .

"Stop shaking," he muttered to himself. "Get a goddam grip." He was on his way to Hosteen Tsinajine's hogan out on the Nageezi road. He thought he knew where he lived. But right now, he felt, yes, like he was losing his mind.

Twenty minutes later he was sitting in Hosteen's hogan, still shaking. Tommy had only met the shaman once before. Hosteen Tsinajine was what the Navajos called a Ná'dleehí, a person who was neither all male or all female, but a third gender which encompassed both, or dual spirits. His gender was fluid. He was dressed now in one of the traditional full skirts, a ti'aakai that many older Navajo women wore. This one was velvet and had been embellished with ribbons. The skirts had become adopted by many females after the Long Walk when Navajos were forcibly removed in 1864 and made to walk the nearly four hundred miles to Fort Sumner.

Hosteen Tsinajine took the news of Tommy's uncle and aunt's death calmly. He did not seem shocked. But, of course, one could not tell with many of these old people. His soft, somewhat pale skin had resisted wrinkles. Tommy then showed him the drawing Wynnie had given him. There was no exclamation. No sound at all. He stared at it for what seemed like several minutes before looking up at Tommy.

"You say Wynnie Haloke gave you this, and she's working with the archaeology people?"

"Yes, Hosteen. She copied the design from an artifact they found on this dig."

"And they're working out by the Gray Mesas?"

"Yes, sir."

Hosteen Tsinajine bent over closer to the piece of paper. He was rail thin, and his back humped almost grotesquely like Kokopelli, the flute player in Hopi Indian stories and often inscribed on rock walls.

"This piece of pottery, sacred pottery, with this drawing of the rainbow did not come from Gray Mesas."

"You know that?" Tommy asked. He immediately regretted the question.

The old man slid his eyes toward Tommy. They were open just a slit, but the black of those two slits was like the edge of an obsidian knife. It cut deeply.

"I know," he repeated. And that was all he said. The words cut through Tommy. He felt a chill run up his spine, and he began to shiver again.

The old man cackled a bit.

"What's wrong? Coyote walk over your grave?"

"Uh . . . no, sir, I don't think so." Tommy inhaled deeply. "About the funeral?" he asked.

"Yes, what about it?"

"I mean for both my uncle and my aunt together, I suppose."

"Of course, together."

"Yes," Tommy replied softly.

"Neither Edgar nor Alice will need to wander back to find each other. In this sense they are lucky. My mother, she comes back."

"She does?" Tommy asked.

Hosteen Tsinajine sighed and nodded. "Yes, just sometimes. My birthday, sometimes her birthday. It's no bother really. She just wonders when I'll be coming."

Tommy was silent for a while.

"But where should we have the funeral for Uncle Edgar and Aunt Alice?"

"The Gray Mesas. The cliffs. Where the chindi won't go."

Of course, Tommy thought.

The Navajos had many ways to ensure that no chindi trailed in the wake of the dead. They were even known to put them on platforms in trees to elude these bad spirits. In this treeless country of the Bisti Badlands, it was normally the cliffs with their Juniper and the ponderosa pine that sequestered their dead as there were so few trees in the flatlands.

"I shall pass the word to the other shaman and medicine men about the funeral." Hosteen Tsinajine paused. His eyes softened. "If that is all right with you, Hosteen Tso."

Tommy was taken aback. No one, no elder with power like that of Hosteen Tsinajine, a medicine man or any shaman, had ever addressed him as Hosteen before. He had no such status in the Navajo community. He was just handsome Tommy who had often chased mostly white girls, out for a quick buck or a quick fuck, smart as a whip. He was the first Navajo in this area to get a realtor's license, and now a revered tribal elder was asking his permission to inform other respected elders of the funeral plans for his aunt and uncle.

"Yes, Hosteen," Tommy whispered. "Yes. It is all right with me. Thank you."

He stood up and walked out of the hogan. Within those scant minutes with the shaman it was as if something significant had changed within him. He remembered some words his grandmother had told him once. An old Navajo saying: "Listen to me, grandson. No river can return to its source, yet all rivers must have a beginning."

He felt in that moment that he was at a beginning, a brand-new beginning.

FOURTEEN

Georgia took David McAlpin into the slot canyon the following day. There seemed to be endless interior paths which they could follow, and Georgia had become quite proficient at finding her way through the rock maze.

"What's that?" McAlpin said as he lifted his binoculars when they emerged from a tunnel at the northwestern end of the slot.

"You see something over there?" Georgia asked.

"A procession of some sort," McAlpin said and handed her the binoculars.

She looked through them, studying the procession.

"I believe it's a funeral procession."

"A funeral out here? How can you tell?"

"I can see two boards with bodies wrapped in burlap."

"But where are they taking them?"

"To those high cliffs over there. That's where the tallest trees grow."

"For burial?"

"It's the Navajo way. I've seen this once before." She paused. "Not always but often they bury the dead in trees, and especially out here in this wild country." She lowered the binoculars. "It looks like they are sweeping the path with brooms, or something." She said, recalling Flora Namingha's funeral, the first Navajo funeral she had ever attended the year before in Taos. "They do that so the dead can't follow their footprints back." She paused again. "But I wonder who died?" She raised the binoculars again. "Oh dear, it looks like we have company."

"Who are they?" McAlpin asked.

"It's Wynnie – the girl who cooks for the archaeology fellows and helps with the excavation as well. You know her." She paused. "She was the one who discovered the potsherds that they were so excited about." She paused once more. "Tommy Tso is sort of a man about town and into real estate."

Georgia and McAlpin continued on their way until they came to the site of the antlers. "Real beauties, aren't they?" Georgia said, turning to McAlpin.

"I'll say."

She began to set up her easel and hoped the wind would stay down.

"The figures of the people walking along that ridge make a nice photo. Look how their shadows slide down the face of the rock."

"Yes, odd, isn't it? Like a march of silhouettes. Almost like spirits themselves." Georgia squinted in the direction that McAlpin was pointing. "Makes the slope below look like there's a picket fence. A picket fence of people."

McAlpin walked on and Georgia picked up her palette to start painting. She squinted one more time at the ridge. "Two pickets left behind?" She whispered the question. The figures appeared to be scrambling down the cliff side. Stragglers, she wondered. Then they turned in the opposite direction and simply vanished. She kept watching for several more minutes. How could they have vanished so quickly? Had they fallen into a slot canyon? It was as if they had just vaporized into the very thin air out here. Or had they only been a mirage? Mirages were common out here. They were an optical illusion created by the refraction of light by heated air that rippled the surface of the ground, or in this case possibly the rock cliffs.

Again, Georgia went back to painting and concentrated on the shapes between the spread of the antlers' tines. Those spaces so perfectly framed the sky. She wished for no clouds. Clouds would ruin the beautiful geometry that appeared to grasp the blue of the sky. She spent an inordinate amount of time painting the antlers. She hoped that a big wind would not come up, for if it did, she'd have to quit. Sometimes the wind surprised her and could send her easel cartwheeling across the desert terrain. It wasn't like when she took the Model A to paint. She had an entire mini studio she could set up in the back of the car and then simply swivel the driver's seat around to paint protected from the wind. Ryan had worked that little miracle for her. It was a godsend.

She was happy that McAlpin had found something else to occupy his attention rather than the antlers. She had considered taking them back with her this time, but for some reason she was still inhibited. She had this uncanny sense that Juan had picked them out for her. And yet she resisted taking them back. They needed to remain where they were—at least for now. Whenever she visited this site, she sensed Juan Nez's presence. It was so strange and yet in an odd way comforting.

Wynnie was experiencing a strange feeling as she walked beside Tommy up the cliff path. Were the chindi following them? Something felt very wrong. If it were the chindi, then she might become afflicted by the ghost sickness. Was this because Tommy's aunt and uncle had both died together in the hospital, and not in their hogan? Had there been a mist after they had breathed their last? She had insisted that Tommy go back to the hogan to check if there were any signs of chindi fever. The fever was a mist that could rise after the death of someone and was often a sign that the ghosts of the dead were clinging to earth.

She stopped and turned to Tommy. "You think maybe they wanted something they had left behind? Tommy, you know to die in a hospital is not right, not good. Like to die in water is not good."

"It's not good to die anywhere, Wynnie. Stop worrying."

But she couldn't and now as she walked in the long line for the funeral, she kept looking back. She felt something was watching them, all of them. There was no mist. No chindi, but what was it?

Georgia and McAlpin had just returned to camp when Orville dismounted his horse having returned from his trip to town for supplies.

"Want me to help you peel those potatoes for dinner?" Georgia offered.

"Sure, and I nearly forgot three letters for you. Picked them up at the trading post."

He handed them to her. One was from Ryan, another from Stieglitz and the third from her sister Anita. Her sister was a wonderful correspondent, with delightful turns of phrase, keen observations, and delicious gossip.

As soon as Georgia finished peeling the potatoes she retreated to her tent and began reading the letters. Ryan's was short and to the point—he missed her. When might she be back? Would she be up for another camping trip with him to White Sands? "Seems only appropriate, Georgia, that after going to the Black Place we should go to White Sands." She had been itching, if that was the right word, to see those gypsum dune fields of the Tularosa Basin for years.

The sun was sinking fast but, as she opened Stieglitz's letter, his flowing script seemed to leap across the page.

My Faraway one,

It was a marvelous evening on the lake. The moon trembled on the horizon like an immense silvery bubble.

I miss you, dearest. And I have good news. Remember the Oppenheimers, the New York people whose sons both went to the Ethical Culture School? Well, their two sons are now all grown up and have bought a home in New Mexico. They say that they are interested in buying one of your paintings. They feel it will 'fit'. When a client uses that word 'fit', I often wonder what they really mean. It's not like a dress, or really anything to do with size.

I feel as if you are almost here beside me in the great stillness of this evening. You are as fine as the white and silvery night—yes, your soul is that fine. And, unfortunately, the world is a hard place for fine souls . . .

He had closed the letter with more descriptions of the beautiful silvery night at Lake George. Georgia sighed softly to herself. When she finished reading the letter, she folded it and replaced it in the envelope.

As was so often the case with Stieglitz's letters—unlike Ryan's—they restored her. She wanted to go out into the night. The moon rising in the east seemed to be coming just to her, as if sent by Stieglitz himself. She loved the idea that she and Stieglitz were perhaps sharing this moon. Did that mean she was being unfaithful to Ryan? No, they were both complicated men, complicated in different ways. Their complications intrigued and inspired her. She needed them both in her life. Ryan almost understood this. Stieglitz never would.

Georgia went out of her tent and fetched Dottie from the hitching post.

"Going out now?" Orville asked.

"Just for a bit."

"Want company?"

"No, just need to be on my own for now."

She wasn't sure why she never thought of this before, but she wondered what those antlers would look like in the moonlight under this full moon, with perhaps stars hovering on the tips. She would save reading Anita's letter until she got back.

It was an exceedingly hot night as she rode out from camp. It was almost as if she could feel the heat being released from the earth. This would make sense, for the earth here was composed of black volcanic soil and rock. Black absorbed heat. Same reason why it was better to buy a white automobile out here than a black one—so you didn't cook yourself to death. The heat now freed from the ground appeared to ripple the air, slightly distorting the darkness. But above the stars hung in what seemed like disorder, as if they hadn't quite settled into place. Unruly kindergarteners resisting lining up for recess.

"Oh, Coyote," she whispered into the wind. "Are you shaking out your blanket again?" She moved forward in her saddle and rested her hands on the pommel, then leaned into the darkness. "What mischief are you up to, foolish creature?"

The night suddenly became cool. There was a new keenness in the air and, as she peered into the darkness, she could swear that the air itself appeared to tremble as a mist seemed to rise like spume from a breaking wave. But this was one of the driest places on earth. It was a desert. She watched the mist continue to rise and it seemed to fold in upon itself. It became a murmuration of sorts, like an enigmatic formation of starlings when hundreds, if not thousands, of birds swoop through the sky in ever-changing configurations as if of one mind. She had seen only one such murmuration in her life while standing in a field in Sun Prairie, Wisconsin with her brother Francis.

"Must be a peregrine falcon up there," Francis had said matter-of-factly. That was Francis's way. He had a mildly authoritarian manner of speaking. "Deception strategy. Confuses prey," he added.

"Don't they ever bang into each other?" Georgia had asked.

"Oh, Georgia!" He'd laughed.

Hola!

But it wasn't Francis speaking now. It was a voice from the mist. From the fog that was beginning to dissolve. All was dark now. It was as if the moon and the stars had been swallowed. Yet less than twenty feet ahead of her, a silver shadow loomed.

Hola, señora . . .

It was then that she saw him.

"Juan," she whispered.

A wraith-like figure melted out of the mist and shadows. An eagle feather seemed to tremble in the high crown of his Navajo hat in a non-existent breeze . . .

Just for you. I found it . . . the antlers.

"Just for me," Georgia whispered.

For you . . . But the words were swallowed as the night faded and that last star still quivered on the edge of the coming dawn.

A new calmness washed over her. *He is not here*, she thought, *but he is at peace.*

FIFTEEN

Wynnie Haloke could not get the funeral out of her mind. Someone had been watching the procession. Was it chindi? But then like mists of chindi it evaporated. There were kivas over by Chaco Canyon that had been discovered in the last fifty years—almost accidentally when a canyon wall fell away and revealed an entire pueblo and not one but several kivas. Had these chindi disappeared into one of these cavities that can form near cliffs? What had disturbed the chindi? Why? If the chindi were aroused, it was not a good sign. But why was she the only one who saw them?

That night Wynnie could not sleep again. She sat up in her sleeping bag and decided that she had to leave this place, but she would not leave it without the potsherd. And she would have to leave on foot. However, it was just five miles into Far Cry. That didn't bother her. No one ran like Navajos. Hadn't she won the race at her Kinaaldá ceremony, the coming-of-age ceremony for girls. That was six years ago, but she was even faster now. Her legs were longer, her speed greater.

The artifacts were in the catch boxes in order by date. She quickly found the one with the rainbow arc that she had found in her screen. Tucking it in her pocket, she stepped out of the cataloging tent and looked toward the sky. Her own star, Náhookòs Bi'áád, was rising in the constellation the white people called Cassiopeia. The stars were with her and the wind. She began to run. Within half an hour she was in Far Cry pounding on Tommy's door.

"What the fuck?" Tommy, bleary-eyed, opened his front door to find Wynnie panting.

"I know it's late."

"Good lord, Wynnie, what are you doing here at . . ." He glanced at his kitchen clock. "Two thirty in the morning?"

"Running away."

"Running away from what? What the hell are you talking about?"

"You know when we walked the path on the ridge for the funeral of your aunt and uncle?"

"Yeah, what about it?"

"I felt, well, I thought I saw chindi following the procession."

Tommy blinked, confused.

"The chindi are restless, Tommy. Believe me."

"Chindi? Are you crazy, Wynnie? You really believe in chindi?"

She nodded. He stared at her with disbelief.

"Yes, I do. So, I ran from the digging site, and I got the potsherd with me."

"What? You have it with you now? The one with the rainbow arc you told me about?"

Now Wynnie had his attention.

"What are you saying, Wynnie?"

"I don't know what is going on, but I certainly know that we're disturbing something with this dig."

"It's late. Let's talk about this in the morning. Come to bed."

Tommy had long fallen asleep but Wynnie couldn't sleep. She got up to make herself a cup of tea, then wandered around Tommy's house. It was a nice house, small but comfortable. There were some family pictures and then some rather nice photographs of landscapes. Mostly desertscapes and some very lovely ones from the seasons of desert bloom. She sat down at his desk. On top was a stack of what must be client folders for real estate agreements, along with some pamphlets and brochures for new properties for sale. She noticed that one had a label that said Phelps. *Oh God*, thought Wynnie, *is Mrs. Phelps actually thinking of buying something out here?*

There was a sheet of lavender stationery, scented at that, and there were three initials engraved at the top in an elaborate font: *MPA*. And the words: *Bridlemere Farm*. The letter began with "My Darling Tommy".

"Darling Tommy . . ." Wynnie whispered to herself. Well, Mrs. Phelps calls a lot of people "darling". She calls Lucille darling. Wynnie sighed, then blinked. But the initials at the top of the page weren't right. It should be *RP*. What's M? What's A? This wasn't Regina Phelps' writing but some other Phelps. But it was from Bridlemere. Wynnie knew that Regina had a horse farm in Virginia called Bridlemere. She cupped her hand over her mouth as she read on:

> *The property you mentioned to me out there in Las Velas, your description is beautiful, and you say it is very near another house that you own in Farmington? So, I am thinking of flying out there to take a look at that property and a few others you mentioned—and, yes, talk to Regina to see if I might get a loan from her against my future inheritance.*
>
> *Wasn't it a blessing when she had to fly out for her grandmother's funeral? Those four days with you were heaven. And guess what . . . well guess what, but do not worry, I was four days late but then relieved. So, no bambino. But maybe someday, Tommy, someday . . .*

Wynnie gasped and held her hand over her mouth. Her first instinct was to run into the bedroom and wake him up. But no, she wouldn't do that. Instead, she very calmly picked up a pen and scrawled a message—*Fuck You*—and walked out the door.

SIXTEEN

It was close to dawn before Georgia opened the letter from her sister Anita. Her encounter with Juan, if that was what one could call it, had left her jittery. She had almost forgotten the letter from Anita and now dug into her satchel to retrieve it.

Dearest Georgia,

We are in Palm Beach as usual in off season as we prepare the house for "hurricane season". I like it here during the off season. The manic social life in January and February can be a little overwhelming. And Robert, being the meticulous person that he is, insists on overseeing the work to prepare the house for the hurricanes. And now he needs to be here as we are actually adding a few rooms to accommodate the Duke and Duchess of Windsor . . .

"What!" Georgia almost screamed. "Why in the hell would you do that?" she muttered and continued reading.

Robert finds them much more compatible than the Kennedys, our next-door neighbors as you might recall. What a rowdy bunch they are. God knows how many children they have. All flaming redheads and they play rowdy games on the beach—touch football, they call it. But guess what? The football managed to "touch" the window in one of the downstairs bedrooms and break it last winter. They were most apologetic, and their father sent some of the sons over to fix it. They were quite well behaved, and even charming in an Irish way. The mother, Rose, sent a cake over that her cook had made. Anyhow, I am just imagining how we might be having drinks on our terrace with the Windsors and a football could come sailing through and knock the Duke or the Duchess on the head . . .

"Would serve them right," Georgia growled. This letter called for "a course correction" as Stieglitz would say and not for the wayward football. What in the world would attract her sister and brother-in-law to the Windsors? She started writing a letter to them that she would take to town that morning and mail.

Dear Anita,

I am absolutely shocked that you are building on to your lovely home in Palm Beach to accommodate the Windsors. I find them both appalling. As a matter of fact, I met her ladyship prior to her marriage to the Duke at Mabel Dodge Luhan's home in Taos and found her loathsome . . .

Three miles away at the Yale encampment, Professor Douglas Acheson slid open the "catch boxes" of the portable filing cabinet that would be shipped back to New Haven. He was frustrated. Where could that potsherd have gone, the one they had found with the rainbow carving? He knew that Wynnie was meticulous in keeping the catch boxes in order. Another graduate student, Ralph, had been giving a lecture that morning to some first-year students pointing out the differences between their find and some artifacts that were dated much later, similar to those from Chaco Canyon sites. Perhaps Ralph had replaced them in the wrong drawer. This was extremely frustrating for Acheson as he had been taking pictures of the finds of this summer to show in his introductory lab course. It was one of the most popular courses on campus. But they had not all been photographed yet. What would he do now? There was nothing like holding the real thing in one's hand. One could almost feel the years, the culture, the hands that had crafted this one small piece of a rich history.

SEVENTEEN

Lucille Samuels regarded Wynnie Haloke as she washed the front window of the trading post. She had shown up in the morning and went to work. She gave no reason, and Lucille knew that it was never good to pry too much with Navajos, or any kind of Indians out here.

Wynnie was wearing a very grim expression.

"Didn't like working out there at the Yale site." It was a comment more than a question.

"Not really," Wynnie growled.

Don't ask why was written all over her face.

However, truth be told, the whole town with fewer than two hundred people seemed a bit off and grim. The shocking deaths of Edgar Adahki and his wife, Alice, had set the town on edge.

Lucille looked over at Pablo, who was sorting the cartons of candy bars that had just arrived. Pablo did not look on edge. He looked angry.

"What's eating at you, Pablo?" she asked.

"Nuthin'."

"Is it the candy? You want to take a couple with you?"

He looked up at her and gave a scowl. "Nooo," he said with a tinge of impatience in his voice and a withering gaze. As if chastising her for having such a thought.

"Well, something's eating at you." She paused. "Still Juan?"

Pablo jumped up. "What do you mean *still*?" The child seemed ready to explode with anger.

Lucille sighed and turned to greet Georgia as she walked through the front door.

"Everybody's touchy around here," she said to Georgia who was holding a letter in her hand and looked rather grim herself. "Even you, Georgia. You look a bit out of sorts."

"Sorry," Georgia said.

"Bad news?"

"Not really. Maybe just frustrating news."

"Well, welcome to Far Cry. Everything seems a little out of whack here," Lucille replied.

"Why's that?" Georgia asked.

"Both the Adahkis died almost at the same time. Whole town is on edge."

"Oh yes, I heard about that. The shaman and his wife. And then I saw the funeral procession going up the cliffs to the west."

"Yep, that's where they bury them. You know the people out here are very superstitious. Don't want any ghosts—chindi—trailing them, and of course don't want the buzzards picking at them."

"How do they fend off the buzzards?"

"They put them high up in those Ponderosa trees, wrapped in heavy-duty canvas tarpaulin." She nodded towards a wall stacked with rolls of fabric. "You couldn't cut that stuff with a buzz saw."

Georgia leaned around and glanced at the fabric rolls. She caught a glimpse of Pablo. He looked angry. His thick black eyebrows crashed into each other. His mouth was pulled into an ugly grimace. It was not mourning she saw but fury. She walked over to him.

"And you're thinking about Juan, right?"

He looked up at Georgia. Tears spilled from his dark eyes. He jumped up and hugged her around the waist. Burying his face in her shirt, he began to sob silently. He was speaking but Georgia couldn't understand the words. His entire body was shaking.

"You wanna go into the back room?" Lucille asked softly.

"Sure," Georgia replied. "Come, dear. Come with me."

She guided Pablo into the room and sat down on a low stack of unpacked boxes.

"You go ahead and cry, child. Cry it out and then I want to tell you something. Something special." She had completely forgotten about her frustration with her sister Anita. It was rather minor compared to Pablo's anguish about Juan.

Pablo sniffled and snorted and after a few seconds stepped

back from her, wiping his nose on his shirt sleeve. "What . . . what do you want to tell me?"

"Well, I think I found something that Juan left for me."

"He left you something?"

"I can't exactly explain it; you have to see it." She inhaled deeply. "Do you think your aunt would allow you to come out with me to where I have been painting for a couple of days?"

"Maybe."

"I can tell her that I need an assistant."

"For what?" His eyebrows crashed together again.

"Well, I'll teach you how to mix paints and help me prime a canvas."

"What does that mean, prime a canvas?"

"I'll teach you. It means getting a canvas ready for me to paint a picture. I just don't slap paint on a raw surface, you know."

"Worried, Regina?" Douglas Acheson looked over at her as they drove into Far Cry.

"Not worried really, just annoyed."

"Can I take a guess?"

"Sure."

"Marya?"

"Indeed." Regina sighed. "She wants to borrow against her inheritance."

"Doesn't she have enough money already?"

"One would think, but lo and behold, last night Lucille drove out here not only with the supplies you ordered but also a telegram for me from Marya. She's coming to Far Cry and wants to talk to me." She paused. "But when is it enough for that girl?"

"Ah well, you know kids." Acheson sighed.

"Yeah, well, I don't know what to do about this kid."

"You meeting her at the trading post?"

"No, actually, if you could let me off at Lottie's café, that would be good." She sighed. "At this point I wish Lottie's was a bar and not a coffee shop."

Two minutes later they pulled into Lottie's.

"I'll be going back in about an hour. Will that give you enough time?"

"God, I hope so." She sighed and got out of the car.

She spotted Marya at a table inside. Marya jumped up and threw open her arms with a joyful cry.

"Regina! You sweet thing."

Regina slid into the booth. "So, what brings you all the way out here?"

"Well. I think . . . I think I need a change of scenery."

"A change of scenery from what? It seems to me that you have three changes of scenery—Bridlemere, the house in Leesville, and Palm Beach."

"You know I suffer from hay fever and none of those places are good for me in hay fever season. My doctor tells me that the very best place for me to live would be out here."

"Here in Far Cry?"

"Not right here specifically, but in the desert. Very little pollen."

"So, buy a house out here. I'm sure you could afford it if you sold the house in Palm Beach or the place in Leesville."

"But we're not out of the depression and it would take a while to sell it. So, I was just wondering if I could borrow this money against my inheritance."

Regina looked at her narrowly. Her first instinct was to say no immediately. But first instincts were not always the best instincts. There was no way this grim, spoiled little girl was going to get a cent out of her. She took a deep breath and smiled.

"Please explain."

"Well, I went to see Bruce Hamilton, the lawyer . . ."

"I know who Bruce Hamilton is," Regina snapped.

"He said that I could talk to you about borrowing some money."

"Yes?"

"Well," Marya went on. "Would you be willing to lend me some money for the time being?" She looked quite innocent with her puppy eyes, but Regina wouldn't fall for it.

Regina knew she needed to play this very cool. Marya was

used to being spoiled by her father, but Regina liked to think that her late husband had left all his money and assets to her out of unconditional love, knowing that he also wanted to teach his daughter a life lesson. And who was she to interfere with this?

"Well, Marya," she said, reaching across the table and taking Marya's hand. "I want you most of all to be healthy, and of course happy. But I'll have to think about it." She took a breath and plastered a small smile on her face. Nothing too enthusiastic, but definitely sympathetic.

This was so like Regina. It infuriated Marya. She had seen her use the smile with her father. He fell for it every time.

"Now how did you get out to Far Cry?" Regina asked.

"Oh, I have a friend out here. Lives in Farmington."

"And they will pick you up?"

"Yes, very nice of him." She took a deep breath. "But please, Regina, think about this."

"Of course, dear. I am not an impulsive person. I want to think on what your father would say to this request."

Like hell you do, thought Marya.

Marya followed Regina out the door of the café.

"One minute, Regina! I don't think you're taking me seriously here. I want what I'm entitled to and you can't take that away from me!"

Regina turned around and looked at her stepdaughter's angry face.

"I told you that I would think about it," Regina replied.

"I don't think you will and I know your answer already."

"Marya, please. You are making a scene. Can we talk about this later?" Regina was about to turn away again, but Marya grabbed her arm—tightly.

"No! We'll talk about this now!"

"Let go of me!"

"Why are you such a bitch?"

"*I'm* the bitch? You are an entitled, spoiled brat."

"Ha!"

Regina turned around, leaving her seething stepdaughter behind, and walked quickly back toward the trading post.

There was no one there when she walked through the door. She turned around so she would have a view from the window, hoping to see the person picking up Marya. A car soon pulled up in front of Lottie's café. A heavy-set man stepped from the car. Not someone she had ever seen before in Far Cry. But then again, he wasn't from Far Cry but Farmington.

EIGHTEEN

Sheriff Ryan McCaffrey pushed open the door of Mr. Q's Barbecue in Albuquerque. In the window was a blue eagle emblem of the National Recovery Administration indicating that the restaurant's owner supported the New Deal. Mr. Q, a Chinese immigrant whose family had come to the United States originally to work on building the railroads, had advanced rapidly in his business life. He now served the only Chinese food in the state of New Mexico. His specialty was barbecued goat "Shanghai style". The menu had a drawing of a goat in a ten-gallon hat.

"Ni hao, Mr. Cop." Jimmy Quan greeted him. "Mr. Judge in the back corner. Your usual table."

"Great, Q, thanks."

Ryan made his way to the corner booth.

"Greetings, sir." Judge Harry Miller tipped his hat as Ryan sat down.

"And which hat are you wearing today, your honor?"

"Not that one."

"So, which one?"

"You don't want to guess?" The judge paused for a second. "Hey, how are you and your girlfriend doing?"

"You mean Georgia?"

"Unless you got a new one."

"Nope, but can you try and be a little more discreet, Harry?"

"Me, indiscreet? I'm a judge, for Crissake. I'm the soul of discretion."

"I never knew that was a requirement for a judge, but if it is, you flunk. So, what's on your mind? Wait, forgive me, which hat is it?" Ryan asked.

"Cultural anthropology and a dash of archaeology."

"Sounds like a spicy soup."

"Possibly. A little too much salt in it."

"Huh?" Ryan replied.

"That's a pun. You know what a pun is, don't you?"

"Of course I know what a pun is," Ryan replied somewhat testily.

"I mean someone is salting a site. A sacred site," Harry said.

"You mean adding relics from another place to increase the value of a dig site—a scam, a confidence trick?"

Harry nodded. "You got it, my friend."

"And where is this happening?" Ryan asked.

"Up north and west in the Bisti Badlands."

"You're kidding, Harry," Ryan replied.

"No, I'm not kidding. What's so funny about it?"

"That's where Georgia is now. It's one of her favorite places to paint." He paused a second. "Now there's some archaeological team from Yale nearby."

"Yes, I know that," Harry replied. He looked deadly serious.

"At least some were from Yale," Ryan continued. "Separate camps, but Orville Cox from the Ghost Ranch was helping Georgia and her people out. Ansel Adams and some other guy, who were out there for art, I guess you would say, and not archaeology. Not really connected to the archaeologists. Georgia calls it the Black Place. She loves to paint out there."

Lily Quan, Mr. Q's daughter, came to take their order and they both went quiet.

"So, what will it be, gentlemen?" Lily asked.

"Well, Lily, I'll have the cowboy-style barbecued pig knuckles," Harry said.

"And I'll have the Bamboo Garden burger with a side of Peking-style noodles." Ryan looked up at the girl. "By the way, what is Peking style?"

"I dunno, I was born here—Grand Junction, where Dad had his first restaurant."

"Never been to Peking?" Ryan asked.

"No. And don't want to go." She gave a quick smile.

"Tell us where you want to go, Miss Lily?" Harry prompted.

She smiled and dipped her head shyly. "Go on, Lily," Ryan urged.

"Stanford, sir."

"And she'll get in!" Harry boomed.

When Lily left the table, Harry leaned across and whispered. "She'll get in. Smart as a whip, that one!"

"So, Harry, continue please with this salting thing. How did you get tangled up in it? Not exactly in your bailiwick, is it?"

"Well, I don't know much except this fellow from up there in Far Cry came into my office here in Albuquerque with a potsherd and said he was sure that they came from a sacred site. The only explanation I could come up with was that it had been transplanted to a legal site that was now being excavated by Yale university. In short—"

Ryan broke in. "They salted an existing site that was not on sacred Navajo lands where they could dig." Ryan scratched his chin and settled back in his chair. "Not the first time and most likely not the last. Happened over in Utah a couple years back. Rather funny really, not involving Indians at all—Mormons."

Harry's usually calm gray eyes had a sudden glint. "What? A kind of 'Joseph Smith slept here' sort of thing?"

"Oh no, much better. The Angel Moroni left some gold plates. You know like the ones discovered back east or something. It turned into a big racket." Ryan gave a chuckle.

"When was this?"

"Just a few years ago. Not in my district so I didn't pay much attention. So, who was the fellow who brought the potsherd from the Bisti to you?"

"Tommy Tso," Harry replied.

Ryan scratched his head. "That rings a bell."

"Yeah, a young, smart fellow who is getting into real estate up there. So, he knows the land."

"It's all Navajo reservation up there, isn't it?"

"Not all. And there is some land that is leasable. Tommy Tso is well connected. His uncle was an important, highly respected shaman."

"Was?"

"Yes. He dropped dead a few of days ago when Tommy showed him what I'm about to show you." He paused and inhaled. "His wife did too."

"Did what too?"

"Dropped dead—right after her husband died."

"Thanks. Should I prepare for a heart attack?"

"Don't worry. Actually, Tommy only showed his uncle a drawing of the design that was carved on the potsherd, not the real potsherd."

"And his wife dropped dead too, you say?"

"Yep, but it was at least a few minutes after her husband died, I think."

"And that's supposed to be comforting?" Ryan asked.

Harry was now digging into his pocket.

"Maybe you should call an ambulance before you show me this deadly potsherd."

"Not to worry."

"I'll try," Ryan replied.

Harry opened the handkerchief he had wrapped it in. It looked like any other potsherd Ryan had ever seen, and he'd seen a lot. Harry drew out his pocket pen and held it about a quarter of an inch above the faintly incised design.

"Yeah, I see it," Ryan muttered. "The názbąs."

"What?"

"The sacred design—a rainbow. Hataałii."

"What?"

"Hataałii, a priestly symbol for singer or medicine man. Found often in Anasazi holy sites, pit houses. They would definitely be off limits. Sacred but hard to translate exactly. Baa hą́ą́h hasin is the Navajo term."

"Yes, that's the problem. Someone is digging where they aren't supposed to be digging," Harry muttered.

"And they're trying to pass this off as coming from a legal site." Ryan sighed.

"But see, it doesn't fit," Harry replied.

"How come? You mean the dating of it?"

"You and I both know that there is no absolute way to date this stuff."

"OK, so why do you feel the site has been salted, Harry?"

"It doesn't really fit with the stratigraphy of the site."

"Says who?"

"That I can't reveal. But this sherd is an outlier, so to speak."

"And no one's picked up on this except this one person who gave it to Tommy Tso?" Ryan sighed.

"More or less," Harry said and settled back in his chair.

"And what would be the motive?" Ryan asked.

"Well, the original finder who gave it to Tommy somchow felt there was something suspicious about the piece."

"So, they stole it?" Ryan asked.

"Yes, but not for the money it could bring into the dig. They stole it because they knew it must have been sacred. That the lead archaeologist must have been digging where he shouldn't have."

"And why would the archaeologist be doing that?" Ryan asked.

"Most likely to get more money—for the dig. They already have a terrific source. Some rich lady from Virginia. The Phelps tire lady." Harry sighed. "In any case, it's going to cause trouble one way or the other." He paused. "You ever heard of Hosteen Tsinajine?"

"Oh yeah, he's a powerful shaman up there. Doesn't pay to have him upset." Ryan sighed. "So why are you telling me about all this? It's not exactly my district."

"That's what's good about it. Not your district. You can go up there and sniff around. You can go under the guise of visiting your girlfriend, Georgia."

"Girlfriend? Do you call an almost fifty-year-old woman a girlfriend?"

"Why not? How's your prostate?"

"Jesus Christ, Harry."

"Mine's a little iffy, they tell me."

"Harry, spare me the details."

Lily came up and set down the burger with the side of noodles in front of Ryan and the barbecued cowboy-style pig knuckles for Harry. Ryan felt a bit queasy as he looked at the pig knuckles.

"Eat up, my boy," Harry urged.

NINETEEN

"OK, Pablo, you're doing great work with the gesso. Be sure you go to the very edge of the canvas. That's it. You're getting it, though."

The child seemed completely absorbed in his task. He learned quickly and applied the primer with an even hand.

"No globs, right?" He turned to her and smiled. The first smile since he had arrived.

"No globs." Georgia nodded. "Canvases dry quickly out here. By tomorrow these will be ready, but now we can head out with the ones I did before you came."

She knew he was anxious to see what Juan had left for her. He had, however, restrained his curiosity. Georgia had waited that first day he'd come with her as it was late, and the light would not be good on the antlers. She wanted him to see them when the light was as perfect as it had been for her. So, on the second day, at 5:45 in the morning after a quick breakfast, she patted him on the shoulder. "Pablo, let's saddle up."

A big smile broke across Pablo's face. He was riding his older cousin's Appaloosa mare. Georgia herself was experiencing a mixture of emotions. She was happy of course that Pablo seemed happy, or at least happier. Deep in her gut she just knew that the antlers had been found by Juan for her. His spirit seemed to saturate the place. She felt his presence like some sort of trail—but to what? She was unsure. However, when she first discovered the antlers, and then when she had ridden out the next day to see them again, there was a spirit that seemed to resonate within her. It was the spirit of Juan Nez, she was certain.

She and Pablo had been riding silently on this still morning for almost thirty minutes in the cool morning air. The late-blooming prickly pear cacti dotted the desert with their pink blossoms that were just opening in the growing warmth of the morning. There was an immutable stillness to everything—so still that Georgia almost imagined the whisper of their petals as they unfurled into full bloom.

She said nothing as they rode up the last hill. She wanted Pablo to spot the antlers first. "There it is!" Pablo gasped as he caught sight of the antlers looming in the morning light. Then grasping with his knees Pablo rose up from the horse's back. After perhaps a full minute or more, he turned around toward Georgia.

"For you! He found these antlers for you, Miss O'Keeffe."

Georgia smiled and nodded her head. "I believe so, Pablo. I believe so." Her vision turned blurry with tears. The two words, "for you," resonated in her ears. Pablo had grown very quiet.

"It's like . . . It's like Juan is here, Miss O'Keeffe. Here with us."

"Yes," she whispered. There was an undeniable intimacy in this moment. "And, Pablo, please call me Georgia."

She was unsure how long they remained mounted on their horses simply staring at the antlers as the sun rose. Pablo finally turned around.

"Can I touch it?"

"Of course you can, Pablo."

"But it's yours."

"Nobody owns anything out here, Pablo," she replied, dismounting. "I'm going to put out the sunshade and set up my easel. And this is for you." She handed him a small knapsack.

"What's this for?"

"Painting. You're a painter today, not just me."

"But I don't know how or what should I paint?"

"You'll never know until you try. Have you ever tried?"

"No, not really," he replied.

"Well, try. There are watercolor paints and . . ." She paused. "Oils if you dare." She chuckled. "I have paper for both."

"But I'm not an artist."

"Don't bet on it." She looked him straight in the eyes with a fierce glint and barked, "Try!"

His brow puckered and he rolled his eyes as if to say she must be crazy. He sighed and muttered, "OK." Propping his tablet of watercolor paper against a rock, he glanced about as if deciding what to paint.

"Not a good idea to prop up the paper," Georgia said. "The paint will run. OK if you were doing oils. So lay the tablet flat."

"OK," he muttered again.

She left him to himself. After twenty minutes or so she glanced in his direction. He seemed completely absorbed, but he wasn't painting. He held his brush in the air, not moving.

What was he looking at, she wondered. Looking at or looking for?

Perhaps there was a presence similar to that day when she first spied the antlers, and the night the figure of Juan melted out of the mist and shadows. Pablo turned toward her. "He's happy you found the antlers."

"How do you know this, Pablo? Did you see him?"

"Not exactly. I . . . I felt him."

She walked over to where he was perched on a boulder beginning to paint. She looked at the watercolor. Yes, he had begun painting the antlers, but the antlers had metamorphosed into a human figure. Not any human figure but Juan Nez and his burro walking through what seemed to be a desert fog, perhaps like the mist she had experienced that night when she felt Juan's distinct presence. "He's near, Miss Georgia. He's near." Pablo inhaled sharply. "But he's . . ." He could not finish what he was going to say.

"I know, Pablo. I know." Georgia embraced the boy.

And then Pablo looked straight into Georgia's eyes. "We must settle his spirit." In that moment Pablo seemed old . . . so old, it crushed Georgia's heart.

Regina Phelps had spent a sleepless night. Yesterday two more potsherds—very old, pre-Anasazi—had been uncovered. Not by Wynnie this time, but Robert Myerhouse. Robert was a young, very handsome fellow who came from the wealthy Myerhouse pharmaceutical family. Enthusiastic, good looking and a keen archaeologist, he was absolutely thrilled with his discovery.

"Can't wait to tell my folks about this. All they want me to do is look through a microscope as opposed to digging in the dirt where real treasures can be found."

"Well, glad to have you on our team," Douglas Acheson exclaimed. "I'll be happy to drop your father a note about this discovery. I think it is so detailed and unusual that it will deserve a prominent place in the exhibit for the opening of the new Phelps building that will be complete by this fall." He paused and looked around for Regina. "What do you say, Regina?"

"Oh yes, definitely."

But Wynnie's words about the sacred lands came back to her. Surely, they were not digging on such lands—and yet with Myerhouse's discovery, this was another artefact that bore sacred symbols. Had they unintentionally gone off track somehow? Were they accidentally violating hallowed ground?

She decided in that moment to get a ride into Far Cry. She needed to call Sam Wolfe at Yale. He was on the site committee that determined which sites would be funded and by how much, based on archaeologist applications.

The next morning, Regina hitched a ride into Far Cry with one of the Yale students who made a weekly run to the trading post for supplies.

"Will you need a ride back, Mrs. Phelps?" he asked.

"Not until much later. No need to hang around for me. Lucille can usually get me a driver or run me out there herself." She thanked the young fellow and walked into the trading post.

"Howdy, Mrs. Phelps, what can I do for you?" Lucille greeted her.

"Might I use your phone, Lucille? And please call me Regina."

"Sure thing, Regina," Lucille replied, flashed her a smile, and nodded toward the office.

Regina closed the door to the office and sat down at Lucille's desk.

"Yale Archaeology Paleontology department. How might I serve you?"

"Regina Phelps for Sam Wolfe."

"Right away, Mrs. Phelps."

"Hello, Regina!"

"Sam, sorry to disturb you . . ."

"Regina, how does it go out there? I so envy you. Now you're seeing archaeology up close. Amazing, isn't it?"

"Yes, yes. Listen, I have to talk fast."

Regina pressed the phone closer to her ear. The story of the suspect relics gushed out of her. "No, no . . . the relics are real, absolutely, but possibly from sacred lands." She had described the artifacts in detail.

"You say one has a rainbow inscribed on it?"

"Yes, and then another similar one was found." She began to describe it in greater detail.

He interrupted her: "So not fake artefacts but looted from another site. A sacred site." He sighed deeply. "From what you have described, well, it just doesn't sound . . ." Sam hesitated to say "kosher". What would Regina Phelps know about kosher? "It just doesn't look right to me. The stratigraphy as you described it is all off. And if it truly had the spiral design or the rainbow, they shouldn't have been touching it. You just don't happen upon those things. It has to be a sacred site, and this could get them into a mess of trouble. Perhaps that's why the girl you mentioned . . . what was her name?"

"Wynnie Haloke."

"Perhaps this was why she was nervous. The indigenous people can sense these things." He paused for several seconds. "You know this new method that's in development called radar?" He began to explain.

"It sounds vaguely familiar."

"It's an electromagnetic way of tracking and recognizing objects at a considerable distance. Now just think of this as being useful in terms of time, not just distance, or for sacred and not everyday objects. Of course, I'm speaking figuratively here. But your friend Wynnie, maybe because she is Navajo, could just have a sixth sense, an awareness as good as radar, that registered with her about the sacredness of this particular object."

"But why would Douglas Acheson do this? Violate the sacred site?"

Sam would have to dance around this question a bit. Should he tell her the truth? That Acheson was a mediocre archaeologist. That there had been questions about his work before. Not enough to get him into any real trouble. But digging at a sacred site or salting another site with "extrinsic" artifacts would constitute a serious transgression.

Sam, who was both a geophysicist and an archaeologist, had his doubts about Douglas Acheson. Yet he could not articulate them. He had heard some vague rumors, indiscretions that had swirled through the inner archaeology community, but nothing credible. Sam himself was obsessed with working on radiocarbon dating, which used the principles of physics to learn about the properties of elements and their isotopes. If indeed they could radiocarbon date this object, they could verify its age. He and Willard Libby at the University of Chicago were getting closer every year by measuring the isotopes of carbon in an object. If Regina Phelps had been deceived, she would become the laughing stock of a world she cared very much about. The world of scholars, archaeology, history. Her philanthropy would forever be in doubt if what she suspected was in fact true. She would be looked upon as a dupe, a victim of fraud. Her reputation as a philanthropist would be ruined.

She could not get a concrete answer out of Sam and so, after saying their goodbyes, Regina sighed and hung up the phone.

"Are you OK, Mrs. Phelps?" Lucille stuck her head round the door.

"Yes, fine. Is that young lady Wynnie around?"

"Not right now. I think she might take a few days off."

"Why?" Regina asked.

"Why?" Lucille repeated. She was confused. Why would Mrs. Phelps be interested in a girl like Wynnie? "Who knows? Could be anything. But I think she said she was going to a sand painting ceremony."

"Sand painting ceremony? What's that?"

"It's a healing ceremony that the Navajos believe in. You know, if something is bothering them."

"Was something bothering Wynnie?"

"Well, I don't dig into my employees' problems, but I know that she had some connection with the Adahkis, the shaman and his wife. They both passed away this week." She paused. "They were a great loss to the whole town."

"Oh, I see." Regina paused. "Was she related to them?"

"Most likely, as there are only two hundred folks in this town. Now if you discount the white folks like me, those who are left are probably related in some way or other to each other. But I know she was pretty upset when she came in earlier."

"What do you think was bothering her?"

"No idea. These people keep their thoughts to themselves." She paused. "If they share them with anybody beyond their family, it might be the shaman for a sand painting."

"Hmmm . . ." Regina appeared quite thoughtful while trying to maintain a calm demeanor. But she just had a hunch that it was time for her to leave. Leave now!

"Uh . . . Lucille, you know the man who drove me here from Albuquerque?"

"José?"

"Yes, he had that nice limousine."

"Yes, Mam."

"Well, I just found out that I need to drive to Farmington. Might you call him?" She could catch a plane in Farmington, fly to Albuquerque and then fly east.

"I can sure try."

She was back in a minute.

"About an hour. He'll try for sooner. That's the best he can do. But really, make yourself comfortable. You can sit right out there on the porch."

"Uh . . . well." She flushed, and a worried look crossed her face. Surely Marya was not still around. She had said something about looking at some properties around Farmington or Las Velas.

"Is there a problem, Mrs. Phelps?"

"This is a very private matter, but I'd rather people not know I'm leaving."

"Of course." Lucille nodded as if she understood entirely, which she did not. "I need to be in my office as I have a call scheduled with my daughter in Albuquerque. Boyfriend problems! You know." She rolled her eyes in exasperation. "But you could wait in the barn, nice and cool and shady out there."

"That would be perfect, Lucille, thank you."

Sam Wolfe had just set down the phone after his call with Regina Phelps. He ruminated on what she had just told him. It was troubling. He walked out of his office. There were not many folk around this time of year, but maybe he could catch a colleague of his who was very interested in radiocarbon dating for his own work, and perhaps discreetly inquire about the Acheson dig out in the Bisti Badlands. However, at just that moment his phone rang again. He picked up. It was his secretary.

"Yes?"

"Professor Wolfe, I have a Judge Harry Miller on the phone for you."

"Who?"

"Judge Miller from Albuquerque, New Mexico."

"Never heard of him but put him through."

It seemed rather a strange coincidence—two calls in a row from one of the least populated states in America.

"Sam Wolfe here. What can I do for you, Judge?"

"Well, a young fella—Navajo fella, came into my office just recently and showed me something . . ."

Less than five minutes later, Sam took a deep breath. "You might not believe this, your honor."

"It's not a courtroom. Just call me Harry."

"All right, Harry. But I just received a phone call from one Regina Phelps fifteen minutes ago concerning a questionable find from an excavation out there."

"And who is Regina Phelps?" Harry asked.

"A lady, a very rich lady, who is underwriting an entire excavation in New Mexico."

"And she had her doubts?"

"I guess you can say that, but no proof." He paused. "I have to say, she seemed rather upset."

"Really!" Harry replied.

"I wouldn't joke about anything like this. This is my profession."

"And the law is mine," Harry said. "I'm going to call a friend of mine who will check this out."

"Well, keep me posted please."

"Sure thing."

TWENTY

Wynnie hadn't spoken to Tommy since the evening she had discovered the letter from Marya Phelps. Or rather he had tried to speak to her, but she refused. When he had come into the trading post, she dashed into a back room. When he tried to approach her on the street, she refused to talk to him. She finally agreed to talk when he cornered her at her aunt's house and offered to go with her for a healing ceremony led by shaman Hosteen Tsinajine. Hosteen Tsinajine did not conduct many healing ceremonies these days, so it was somewhat of an honor that he had agreed to perform one when Tommy asked.

"He agreed?" Wynnie said.

"Yes, he did."

"You told him about cheating on me?"

"No, but I did tell him about the potsherd." Tommy paused and inhaled deeply. "Believe me, Wynnie, the potsherd upset him more than . . . than . . ."

"Than what?"

"More than me screwing that stupid girl would have."

"So, what did you tell him?"

"I just said that we both needed healing. I didn't specify why or what. We just both need healing. But I told him also about the potsherd."

"You mean that?"

"I mean it, Wynnie. You can't go to see a shaman with lies."

Healing ceremonies were not cheap. When performed by a shaman as highly regarded as Hosteen Tsinajine, they could cost as much as fifty dollars. Was he saying he'd pay for it? Wynnie turned her head and looked into the distance. How could he have done this to her, slept with this woman? Regina Phelp's stepdaughter. It sickened her. Was it her money? Her beauty? Or just plain sex? Did it even matter? But she had agreed to let him come with her. After all, how would she get there? Run? It was over thirty miles.

Two hours later they were at Hosteen Tsinajine's place. She had first shown him the potsherd she took from the camp. Then he seated her in the middle of a circle inscribed on the ground of the medicine lodge.

Wynnie peered at the stream of pale-yellow pollen dust as the shaman sifted it in a straight line within a square frame of willow branches in the circle. This was, Wynnie thought, to represent the goddess Dsilyi' Neyáni who stood in the House of Dew, a seminal configuration in many sand paintings. That was all that Wynnie really understood about this ritual. She had been to only one sand painting ceremony years before, when she was just a small child, for her great-auntie who had a large tumor growing in her head. Well, now Wynnie had a tumor in her heart and so did Tommy.

The shaman and his assistant began to waft some branches over the painting and when this was completed more sand was deposited, making the picture of an eagle followed by the kátso-yisçàn, or great plumed arrows. That was when Wynnie felt something stir within her.

As she sat in the medicine hogan, the words in that hideous letter on the lavender paper started to fade and a peace finally began to settle upon her. The shaman was now chanting as he sprinkled some more sand, this time a glittering black sand that reminded her of the stars—the stars that were within her, the stars that had first propelled her into the night, the stars with wings with the potsherd in her pocket to bring to Tommy and then the horror of the discovery of the letter from Marya. She clearly pictured their lovemaking. They had both shared flesh with this man. A wave of nausea swept through her. The shaman's assistant offered her a bowl. She vomited. She heard a cry in the background. It was Tommy. He saw his sin now, his violation in the regurgitation in that bowl, and in those moments a healing began within Wynnie.

Then the shaman asked her to sit on the sand painting. She

felt the last of the sickness flow from her and, when she rose, the shaman swept away the sand. The bad spirits were gone. The sickness was vanquished. Order had been restored.

What a strange landscape this was, Ryan mused as he drove along the Old Blanco road. He wasn't quite sure why Georgia was so drawn to the region. But in her peculiar way, with that inner eye of hers—as he thought of it—she had been mesmerized by this landscape. She didn't exactly transform it, but she saw something beneath the surface that tantalized her. Her Black Place paintings were his favorites in an odd way. He was mildly surprised when she told him they were Stieglitz's favorites as well. "Well, black and white, that is essentially his palette as a photographer," she had replied.

This fellow Stieglitz was an eternal mystery to Ryan. He understood the artistic attraction between the two, but beyond that it seemed that they were as different as could be. He might have inspired her as an artist, but he was hurtful to her as well—not viciously so, and perhaps not even intentionally. He respected Georgia but he would always put his own thoughts and interests first. Stieglitz's ego was such that he had little room for anything else. Perhaps he had become jealous. Her income in the last few years vastly surpassed Stieglitz's. Ryan once asked Georgia if Stieglitz's infidelity hurt her. And she just shrugged.

"You don't care?" Ryan had asked.

"I care in my own way." And in her own way Georgia could become instantaneously enigmatic. It was as if she had drawn a curtain and receded into a shadowy, completely unreachable place. A black place, as it were.

Ryan loved her flower paintings, but they lacked, in his mind, the mystery of the Black Place. That mystery, however, the intrigue, was perhaps the same thing that drew him to Georgia. Or was at least representative of that enigma. She was in Ryan's mind a riddle—a riddle, or a puzzle with a riddle, he thought. Two years later Winston Churchill would use the perfect words. Georgia and Ryan would have a feisty exchange. "That's what I said about you—two years ago, before Churchill ever dreamed of saying it!"

"But Churchill said it about Russia, that he couldn't predict what Russia might do. He wasn't talking about me."

"He could have been," Ryan said.

"You never said it to me!" Georgia had countered.

"Well, I thought it. I don't say everything out loud to you, Honey Bunch. Do you tell me every single thought you have?"

"No, but still . . ."

It was unimaginable that Stieglitz would ever call her "Honey Bunch", but for some obscure reason she liked it when Ryan did. She knew she wasn't soft and cuddly as the name implied, but somehow on occasion she wanted to be—just for Ryan. That was the great thing about Ryan: he appealed to aspects of her that she never dreamed she possessed. The first time he ever called her Honey Bunch, she growled. However, she instantly regretted it and turned around, smiling broadly and said, "You can bunch my honey anytime you like!" He laughed now as he recalled her saying this. Ah! He missed her, even though she'd been gone just a few weeks.

In future years he would not be able to recall how the exchange between himself and Georgia had ended about Churchill and Russia. Possibly in bed. Georgia could be a sly flirt. He'd have to keep a low profile out here for now. Better that she did not know he was in the vicinity, if that was possible.

But now as the shadowy landscape whizzed by, he thought of her out there painting in this wild country. He purposely had not come in his cop car or wearing his uniform. The less he looked like the law, the better, so he could see what the hell was going on out here at this dig. There was no formal law enforcement for miles in this area. At least no cops would feel that he was stepping on their toes.

Judge Miller had told him to get in touch with the shaman out here, one Hosteen Tsinajine. The name rang a dim bell with Ryan and, as he turned off the main road onto a rutted track, he tried to place the man's face. He glimpsed a scattering of perhaps a dozen hogans across the land. He had no idea which one might be Hosteen Tsinajine's. He pulled up to the first one and saw someone outside. It was an elderly woman with a burlap bag on her back and a crook in her hand as she tried to guide a small flock of sheep across a dried riverbed.

Leaning out the window, he greeted her. "Yá'át'ééh shimasaní."

"Eh, Yá'át'ééh."

"Can you tell me which way to Hosteen Tsinajine?"

"Take the fork ahead to the left. He has two hogans. He's at his medicine hogan right now. Sand painting today."

"Ahéhee," he replied.

Five minutes later, Ryan saw a tall, lean young man guiding a young woman by the elbow out of a hogan. Behind them came the shaman, Hosteen Tsinajine. Ryan pulled the car over to the side of the road and stepped out.

He walked only a few feet and then stopped. He knew he should let them approach first. Hosteen Tsinajine stepped ahead of the couple and walked directly to Ryan. *Ah*, thought Ryan, *a Ná'dleehí, a two-spirit person, or one of two genders*, as he saw the tall figure approaching in the full tiered skirt.

Ryan introduced himself in the traditional way: "Ryan McCaffrey from the Towering House clan." He stopped, as only his mother was Navajo. His other half was Irish, sons of Godfrey was the clan—a powerful Irish kind of clan, which dated back perhaps one thousand years or more. The clan originated in the Northern Irish county of Fermanagh. Or so his father had told him.

"Aye," the shaman replied. "Hosteen Tsinajine from the Waters Flow Together clan and the One Who Walks Around clan. What brings you here?"

"Perhaps the same thing that brought these young folk here," Ryan offered, nodding at Tommy Tso and Wynnie Haloke.

"Do you know them?"

Ryan shook his head. Tommy began to walk toward them.

"Do you know him?" Hosteen Tsinajine repeated.

"No, but I understand that some Diné laws have been disturbed."

"Violated!" Tommy growled. "You're Sheriff McCaffrey from Santa Fe, aren't you? But not the Navajo police."

"Correct," Ryan answered. "There are no Navajo police here in the Bisti Badlands, not since the last officer was killed."

"That's why we searched out Hosteen Tsinajine," Tommy said curtly.

"And that is also why you searched out Judge Harry Miller, right?" Ryan asked.

"You know him?"

"Very well," Ryan replied.

"Then you understand why we are here with the shaman."

"Not completely."

Tommy turned to Wynnie and beckoned her.

"Let's go to my hogan," Hosteen Tsinajine offered.

TWENTY-ONE

Regina Phelps sank down on a bale of hay. It was cool in the barn. She needed to think things through. Sam Wolfe had seemed, if not unnerved on the phone, then a bit shaken. There was definitely something in his voice that alarmed her. If what Sam Wolfe said was true, or came to be true, she would be profoundly humiliated. Her career as a philanthropist would be tainted forever if she was discovered supporting research on sacred lands. There were two things that Regina cared deeply about: seeing her name on a building, and seeing her flawless face, newly tightened from her second facelift, in the mirror. She knew she was vain, but she felt her philanthropy compensated for her vanity. Her late husband Edward would tease her often about her vanity but never complained. He was such a generous man. After her first facelift, he had quoted Ralph Waldo Emerson: "Vanity costs money, labor, horses, men, women, health and peace, and is still nothing at last; a long way leading nowhere." Then Emerson added, "Only one drawback: proud people are intolerably selfish, and the vain are gentle and giving." Regina reminded herself often that she was gentle, and she was giving. So yes, that made up for her vanity.

But when that first facelift had begun to droop a bit, she suspected Edward's somewhat wandering eye had been cast in the wrong direction, and not on her any longer. To remedy this matter, she got a new facelift and even had breast enhancement, as it was called. He quickly returned to "the fold", so to speak, very apologetic. He left her another million dollars in his will and added her name to the building at Yale alongside his. It now read "The Regina and Edward Phelps Center for Archaeology and Anthropology".

She heard a car pulling up. Then a shadow slid across the barn door.

Regina stood up from the bale of hay and began to turn around. She felt herself being grabbed from behind. A bag was pulled over her head. She gasped. There was a strange odor. *This can't be happening*, she thought. *Not to me . . . not me . . .* She tried to raise her hands to her face, but the person was twisting some wire around her wrists. She was gasping and she tried to scream, but the air was thick with this oddly sweet smell. She felt a numbness creeping through her. She tried to hold her breath to avoid breathing the vapor, but it was useless and with her last deep breath the world went black.

Thirty minutes later the car pulled to the side of the road. There was a deep ditch. The driver lugged the bag with Regina's body and dumped it into the ditch. Then, taking out a knife, he sliced open the bag to make easy work for the coyotes or the wolves. It wouldn't take them long.

After meeting with Tommy Tso and Wynnie Haloke at the shaman's hogan, Ryan drove back toward Far Cry, mulling over what the two young people had told him. As he was driving, he passed another car, stopped at the side of the road. He slowed down and pulled over.

"You need help?" he called out from his car to a figure who was coming up from a culvert that ran beneath the road.

The person just waved at him, their face swallowed by shadows. He couldn't make out if it was a woman or man—they were too far away and the heat made outlines distorted.

"Keep hydrated," Ryan replied cheerfully. "That's the key out here."

Ryan just received a thumbs-up and continued on his way.

TWENTY-TWO

"José! That you?" Lucille Samuels called from her office. "She's waiting out in the barn."

"No, Mam," Ryan McCaffrey called toward the source of the voice.

"Where the devil is that guy?" Lucille murmured to herself as she leaned out of the back office and saw the somewhat heavyset but attractive-looking fellow looking through the selection of Navajo rugs.

"I see you have some Grace Ornelas from the Water's Edge clan and born of the People of the Sacred Spring clan."

"Yes, when the owners of the Old Mission Trading Post retired, I got these at a steep discount. They are hard to come by these days."

"You're telling me!"

"We also have some of Hosteen Tsinajine's rugs. He's a very good weaver, out on the Nageezi road."

"Ah yes, I heard that."

"You should stop by his place. What brings you here?"

"I have some business with that archaeology dig that's going on out in the Bisti Badlands."

"You're not here instead of José to pick up Mrs. Phelps, are you?"

"Mrs. who?"

"Regina Phelps, she came in from the dig and was waiting for a ride to Farmington. I called up José, her usual driver, and he said he'd be here in an hour. Now two hours have passed and he's not here yet. I told her to wait in the barn where it's cooler." She paused for a moment. "I should go check on her."

"I parked right by your barn when I came in."

"Let me go check," Lucille said.

She was back in less than five minutes, a worried look on her face.

"My God, she just up and disappeared on me." Hurrying to the front door of the trading post, Lucille looked out. It was basically a one-street town. She came back with a perplexed look on her face. "She just seems to have vanished."

A car could be heard pulling up to the trading post.

Lucille rushed to the door.

"Sorry, Lucille, I got delayed." José stepped out of the dust-covered limousine. "Mrs. Phelps here?"

"No!" Lucille barked. "I can't figure it out. Where could she have gone?"

Ryan observed this exchange. The name Regina Phelps was vaguely familiar to him. Had Judge Miller mentioned her name when they had lunch, something about the dig being financed by some rich lady from back east? Possibly. He didn't want to ask to use the phone in the trading post. Luckily, he had brought his two-way police radio that was set up in his car.

Five minutes later he had Judge Miller on the radio.

"Regina Phelps?" Harry said. "Oh yes, she was bankrolling this operation."

"You mean the dig."

"Yep, she and her late husband had a passion for archaeology and ethnography. There's a building named after them at Yale."

"Well, she's kind of disappeared."

"Disappeared? She was out there?"

"I guess so."

"You mean you now got a missing-person case on your hands?"

"Maybe so. I'll have to . . ." Ryan hesitated. "Dig into this a bit more, pardon the pun."

"Indeed, put on your archaeologist hat and keep me posted."

Ryan hung up. *My archaeologist hat?* he wondered to himself.

He walked back into the trading post.

"Mam, by any chance, is the archaeology dig out there the one from Yale?"

"Why yes, it is," Lucille replied.

"Then I'm wondering if an old friend of mine is on it."

"Professor Acheson, you mean?"

"Yep, we go back a bit."

"Oh yes, Douglas Acheson has been coming here for years. Are you an archaeologist too?"

"No, nothing of the sort." That was true at least, but now he was going to launch into his cover story. "I'm a retired dentist. Now just an amateur astronomer, really." That was the untrue part. If anyone was an amateur astronomer in Ryan's world, it was his late wife, Mattie. She knew the stars and he had learned enough from her to fake it a bit.

"It's a good time of year for stargazing," Ryan added.

"Oh yes, if one has the time."

Ryan was about to say he was retired. But then she might ask from what and that would involve more lies.

Half an hour later he had arrived at the site. Lucille's directions had been excellent.

"Howdy," he called out cheerfully to a middle-aged man who was giving instructions to a couple of young men. They were all wearing dark blue hats with an insignia of some sort on them.

The man looked up and came over to Ryan's jeep.

"Can I help you?"

"Oh, just thought I would stop by. I'm out here to stargaze, but I heard about your dig at the trading post. Sounded interesting."

"It is!" the fellow said almost jubilantly. "We're making some amazing discoveries. I'm the head of the dig, Professor Douglas Acheson, from Yale university. You say you're out here for stargazing?"

"I'm just an amateur at best. You like what's in the earth; I like what's above it. But purely as an amateur, mind you. So, I don't think we'll get in each other's way."

"Not a problem, sir," Acheson said warmly. "Plenty of room for everyone out here." He then pointed to the insignia on his cap beneath what appeared to be the Latin words Lux et Veritas: Light and Truth. The motto of Yale University.

"Looks like we're in the same business. Light and Truth. We dig; you look toward the stars. As you said, we won't be in each other's territory."

"Definitely not," Ryan said. "I thought maybe I'd camp over

by that bristlecone tree. Then set up my telescope on top of my jeep. And don't worry, I brought my own water."

"That's a Willys jeep, isn't it?" one of the students asked.

"Yes, a friend of mine lent it to me. Wonderful vehicle. It's perfect for out here."

In truth, that friend was Mabel Dodge Luhan. She had donated two Willys jeeps to the police department. Mabel was an endless source of vital equipment, not just to the police department, but also hospitals in both Santa Fe and Taos.

"Four-wheel drive, isn't it?" Acheson asked.

"Yes, sir."

"Maybe I should ask Mrs—" He chopped off his sentence abruptly.

"What was that?"

"Oh, nothing."

"Well, I think I'll drive over there and set up my camp now," Ryan said.

"Go along, sir, and happy stargazing. What are you hoping to see tonight?" Acheson asked.

"Possibly Mercury. 'Course, as you might guess from its name, Mercury has one of the fastest orbital periods and it should be visible by this time of year." Ryan had no idea what an orbital period was; he had just heard Mattie talking about it once with one of her stargazing friends.

TWENTY-THREE

Ryan McCaffrey had parked the jeep almost half a mile from the Yale camp after a quick tour of the archaeology site where he was confident that he had impressed Professor Acheson with his ignorance of archaeology and Anasazi history. "You don't say . . . well, I'll be . . . And you say you feel that this is one of the oldest places so far discovered?" he commented, he hoped convincingly as Acheson had gone on at some length describing the extraordinary discoveries they had been making, and reaching layers of time that were quite significant, "landmarks" in the archaeology of the southwest.

The problem was that Ryan now realized that he might have also impressed him with his ignorance about astronomy. He was careful to mention that it was his late wife who had taught him all he knew about the stars. A familiar voice echoed in the back of his mind when he mentioned Mercury—this was not a planet he should be looking for at this moment in July.

Ryan, you fool, this is not Mercury's time at all. April and May is when—if you're lucky—you can spot Mercury. It was Mattie's voice in the back of his head. "Goddammit! How could I make such a mistake?" he muttered. *It's the Pleiades, dummy, or Sagittarius, or Corona or Taurus*, Mattie's voice continued to echo in his head as he set up the telescope—crucial to his cover story—on a platform on top of the Willys jeep. The wind blew the strains of a guitar from the archaeologists' camp, punctuated by occasional laughter, and then the howl of a coyote.

As the sky drew darker, and the stars began to melt out of the night, soon all became quiet. The universe stretched above his head. If only Mattie was here to guide him. Often when he would come home late, he would find her on their patio.

If it was July, the scent of the peach tree wafted through the air. She would be out there with her telescope, the most expensive gift he had ever bought her, minding the heavens as she put it, and "dusting" the nebula where newborn and dying stars swirled in an enigmatic astral dance. Oh, how he missed her, and yet how deeply he loved Georgia. *A glutton for love, I am. Take my hand, dear Mattie, and star walk with me through this night.*

Mattie's voice seemed to whisper in his ear. *Look at that!* Ryan found himself escaping the skin of the earth and swept up into the magnificent silence of this starry realm. The breeze had ceased and hung dead in the air, increasing the awesome, primeval silence of the sky. But it was in this silence that he could feel and not hear the two women he had loved: Mattie and Georgia.

Within the shadows of this night, Gideon Blake stood next to Douglas Acheson.

"That jeep over there?" Gideon asked.

"Yeah, the astronomer fellow I told you about. I guess he arrived when you were gone. It's a Willys, no less. Funny, I never got the fellow's name. But he's an amateur astronomer. Come to look at Mercury or something," Acheson said.

"Mercury at this time of year? I doubt it."

"You know about stars?"

"Not much, but I do know that the chances of spotting Mercury at this time of year are nearly impossible."

"Well, maybe he said something else," Acheson said as he took a deep breath.

The moon was slipping away to the west, which meant that the starscape was becoming even more vivid. At the same time, beneath the dwindling light of the waning moon, the shadows of the saguaro cacti began to stretch across the Black Place—black on black. No wonder Georgia liked to come to this place, Ryan thought. She was intrigued by the blackness in the same way that she was intrigued by bones. But, as she once said, they both held intrigue for her, an aesthetic intrigue. And so, she used the apertures in the bones almost like a telescope to frame the cerulean blue of the sky.

She once told Ryan about one of her earlier trips to the Black Place, and how she became attuned almost sensitive to black. She came back to New York and passed a florist that had a display of black irises. She stopped short and almost gasped, for the morphology of the overlapping whorl of sepals enclosing the petals reminded her of a patch of gently cascading hillocks in the Black Place. "Black frightens a lot of people," she had said once in an interview. "Terrifies them, but you have to get beyond the blackness of black and really look. You could really spend your whole life being terrified. It's honestly a waste of time . . ."

Then Ryan recalled her being interviewed on a phone call once, where she was saying to an art critic that terror was a part of life. "I've been absolutely terrified every moment of my life, and I've never let it keep me from doing a single thing that I wanted to do." There was a pause, and he heard her say to the critic on the other end of the call. "Well, to each his own. You see a vagina, and I see an iris. So there."

Then she hung up.

"Holy smokes, Georgia!" Ryan had gasped.

"Oh, let them see what they want." She then paused and began to hum a familiar Gershwin tune as she danced up to him.

> "You like potato and I like potahto
> You like tomato and I like tomahto
> Potato, potahto, tomato, tomahto
> Let's call the whole thing off."

Ryan chuckled to himself, opened a beer and sat back in the chair that he had fastened to the roof of the jeep. He tipped his head toward the sky. He'd rather sit here in his chair and just watch with his naked eye and think—think about Mattie and Georgia. They would have liked each other. Of this he was certain. He didn't need to look at it through a telescope to wrap himself in this lovely star-thick night. He counted himself lucky. Lucky to have been loved by two extraordinary women.

TWENTY-FOUR

"We must settle his spirit," Pablo had said, and the day after Georgia had shown him the antlers, she and the boy had set out to do just that. They both felt Juan to be near where she had found the antlers. Although they increased the circumference of their search for his body, they never lost sight of the antlers, until on the second day of their search, when Georgia was following Pablo, the boy simply dropped out of sight. It was so quick, she gasped and gave a small shriek.

Racing forward, within seconds the ground seemed to crumble beneath her feet. She felt herself falling into a void, and then in another few seconds she came to an abrupt but soft landing.

"Miss Georgia?"

"Pablo! You're . . . you're here?"

"Yes, Mam. You too?"

"I guess." She got to her knees. Pablo was not more than a few feet away.

She looked around. There were walls of deep sand with some protruding rocks. Words echoed in her head. *Toto, I have a feeling we're not in Kansas anymore.*

"It's a sinkhole," Pablo muttered.

"Sinkhole? They're not supposed to be here. Maybe Florida, but not here."

Pablo looked at her with weariness. *Not supposed to be here.* What did she mean? White people were so weird. White people thought they made all the rules. What was she talking about? Not supposed to be here?

"Well, they are here . . . sinkholes, and we're in one," he answered. He was dismayed but unruffled. "Really, Miss Georgia, you think that about sinkholes?"

She looked at him. "You don't think so?"

"I don't know so, like you do." He gave her a withering look which spoke volumes about what she did not know.

"Well, here we are." She sighed.

Pablo nodded.

"What do we do? Any ideas?" Pablo shook his head. But his eyes fell on something.

"What are you looking at?"

"That's a big rock over there . . . like a boulder, maybe." He paused. "But actually, maybe a rock wall . . . I think."

"Sinkholes don't have rock walls. At least I don't think so."

Was this the white person's way of saying maybe they do have rock walls? Pablo wondered.

Miss Georgia was the nicest white person he'd ever met, but sometimes she was just so white. He started to get up and brush off his pants.

"Where are you going, Pablo?"

"To look at this rock."

"Be careful, it might not be safe."

"Nothing is safe, Miss Georgia."

Georgia nodded slightly. Children could make you feel like such a fool. She watched him as he slid his hand behind the edge of the boulder. He then pressed one side of his head against it.

"It's not just a rock," he called to her.

"What is it?"

"A tunnel, I think."

"A tunnel to where?"

Pablo sighed. This was the dumbest question he had ever been asked.

He turned around and smiled at her. "I don't know, Miss Georgia."

"Dumb question, right?"

"Yes, Mam." He laughed softly.

"I know you think I'm stupid, Pablo."

"Not exactly." He smiled.

His smile melted her heart.

TWENTY-FIVE

That same day, Orville Cox walked in the teasing light of dusk toward something odd in the Badlands. At first, he thought the configuration he saw stuck in the sand was an upside down cross, a wandering crucifix of some sort. But as he drew closer, he realized it was a painter's easel.

"Oh no!" Orville gasped as he continued to walk. A sickening feeling began to rise from the pit in his stomach when he came to what had most likely been a deep depression in the earth. But now he could tell that there had been subsequent collapses. "Subsides" they were called. No chance of survival. Georgia and Pablo would have been smothered to death by tons of limestone, salt, and carbonate rock that had been dissolved by hidden streams of groundwater over centuries.

David McAlpin came up to him. "What's this?"

"Death," Orville said as he squeezed his eyes shut. McAlpin started to take a step forward.

"Don't!" Orville roared and grabbed his shirt collar. "It's a sinkhole. We have to back away slowly. It could still cave."

The two men began to walk backwards as if they had been confronted by a rabid beast.

They heard Ansel Adams calling out, "What is it, fellas?"

Orville turned slowly. "Stand back, Mr. Adams. I am afraid what you are seeing is Georgia's and Pablo's grave."

"Oh my God, a sinkhole." Ansel began to waver. McAlpin grabbed his arm.

"Steady there, Ansel."

"We have to get back to town and call this in as an APB," Orville replied.

"APB. What's that?" McAlpin asked, still with a steady grip on Ansel's elbow.

"All-Points Bulletin," Orville answered. "But right now we have to back away carefully and not trigger another one."

"Another one?" Ansel croaked.

When they were perhaps a thousand feet away, the three men mounted their horses and raced off at a full gallop back to town.

"I'll call Oscar over in Farmington. He's the fire chief," Lucille said as the men ran into the trading post to announce what had happened. "They'll put it out on the fire brigade network."

Oscar called other fire departments in the nearby area. Less than an hour later they heard the first sirens splitting the air. The entire population of Far Cry—all two hundred souls—came out to watch the parade of fire engines, police cars, and big machinery including cranes and excavators.

The last star had faded and Venus, the morning star, was just trembling on the edge of dawn when Ryan McCaffrey's radio began to crackle.

"What's got you calling this early?" There was an unaccustomed pause. "Joe, this you calling?"

"Yeah, it's me, Sheriff. Bad news," Joe Descheeni, his top deputy, replied.

The two words struck him as odd. Most police work was "bad news", for it meant that something had gone wrong in some way. In short, it involved incidents that demanded a police response to an event which, if not fixable, could be constrained in some manner. But this was different; this was bad news for a particular person, something that struck close to home for the listener on the other end of the phone. Rather like when Mattie got her cancer diagnosis.

"It's Georgia . . ." Joe blurted it out. "Georgia is missing and . . . and maybe . . . dead." Cool-headed Joe Descheeni's voice cracked when he said the last word.

"No! What?"

"A sinkhole was called in very close to where Georgia was painting in the Bisti Badlands. She and a young kid are missing. They found her easel nearby."

The words jumbled in his mind. Sinkhole . . . Georgia . . . a kid . . . what kid?

Ryan immediately began packing up the telescope and set out from what had been his campsite. As he was pulling out, Douglas Acheson approached him.

"Leaving so soon?" Acheson asked as he passed the archaeologists' camp.

"Emergency," Ryan called out of the car window.

"A star emergency? Didn't know those happened."

"They don't," he said and pressed the accelerator.

Deputy Descheeni had given him the compass bearings for the site of the sinkhole. "Be careful," Joe had warned. "I'll come down as soon as I can."

"Fuck," Ryan had murmured silently. If Georgia was dead, he wanted to be dead too. If a sinkhole had devoured her, he wanted to be devoured as well, and to be buried under tons of sand. It would be a quick death, he knew it. Like an avalanche, only sand not snow. No biblical floods. He had read somewhere that in an avalanche it took victims fifteen minutes before they expired. But with a sinkhole it was probably less.

As he approached the site of the sinkhole, he immediately saw Orville Cox from the Ghost Ranch.

He stopped and hopped out of the jeep.

"So, how long ago did this happen, what do they think, Orville?" Ryan asked.

"They're not sure," Orville replied. "You just happen to be here?"

"Yeah. Other business. How did Georgia get involved in this?"

"She was just out painting, as usual. We found her easel right at the edge of the hole. She was out here with a young kid she's taken under her wing, so to speak. Kid swallowed up too, most likely."

"Who's that fellow over there?" Ryan asked. He pointed to a man who was wearing a pith helmet and crouching by the lip of the sinkhole. He was also wearing a harness of sorts with a long rope attached.

"That guy is from the University of New Mexico, a geologist. Expert on sinkholes, I guess. He thinks there's been one subsidiary slide since the first release."

"Release?"

"Collapse—the first opening."

"Jesus Christ." Ryan wiped his chin. He felt drenched in despair.

TWENTY-SIX

Pablo was right about the opening in the rock wall. It was a tunnel of sorts. They had now been winding through it for several hours. Luckily, they each had canteens in hand when the earth had seemed to slip away from under their feet. Pablo had a pack of Tootsie Rolls stuffed in his pocket. He held out the package.

"Have one," he offered.

"My goodness, Tootsie Rolls. You know, I met Leo Hirschfield once," Georgia replied.

"Who's that?" Pablo asked.

"The fella who invented Tootsie Rolls."

"Must be rich."

"I expect so, like that Mrs. Phelps lady."

"Who's she?" Pablo asked.

"The lady who helps on the archaeology dig out here. Her husband was in the automobile tire business though, not candy."

"Oh, the rich lady in the limousine. Yeah, she came out here. She sometimes brings candy for the kids in Far Cry. Not Tootsie Rolls, but other kinds."

"How generous of her." Georgia did nothing to disguise the sneer in her voice.

"You don't like her?" Pablo said, picking up on her tone.

"Well, I think she could bring something to Far Cry that would serve better than candy—like books or medicine." Georgia paused. "What would you bring to Far Cry if you had lots and lots of money, Pablo?"

"Well, books I guess, and maybe . . . maybe a hospital," he said as they continued to walk the narrow path through the tunnel.

"Yes, a hospital would be a very good idea, and I'm sure Mrs. Phelps could afford it."

"If there were a hospital here, my mother would not have died."

"Oh dear, really? What did she die of?"

"An exploding appendix."

"Goodness."

"Yes, it exploded in my aunt's car five miles outside of Farmington."

"Well, that's too bad. Yes, a hospital would be great out here." Maybe she would mention it to Mabel Dodge Luhan, her close friend in Taos. Mabel had already been incredibly generous. She'd bought an X-ray machine for the hospital in Taos and had spread her wealth across the state so it could reach the neediest communities. So had Mary Cabot Wheelwright, a wealthy Bostonian who had just donated hundreds of thousands of dollars to the new Indian Museum in Santa Fe.

They continued walking in silence.

"You know, Pablo, I have a feeling that this tunnel is winding upward somehow."

"Yeah, me too." He paused. "And the rock looks different." He hesitated. "More like the cliff rocks."

"I think they call this shale. A geologist friend of mine told me that."

"Gee whiz, Miss Georgia, you have a lot of important friends. The Tootsie Roll guy and now this geologist man. What does a geologist do?"

"They study ancient rocks and figure out what was happening thousands and millions of years ago. A kind of scientist."

"See, you know important people, a scientist and a tire maker and a candy maker," Pablo said.

Georgia gave a soft laugh and kept walking. The slope was definitely inclining.

"Hey, guess what I found?" Pablo called out.

"What?"

"A sun dagger."

"Sun dagger? What's that?"

"Come here and see."

Georgia walked fifteen feet or so up to where Pablo stood.

"Rock art?" she murmured, looking at a spiral design carved in the rock.

"Not just that. It's so a sliver of light can cut through the center of the spiral on the longest day of the year. Shį́įgo Shá Ninádááh. That's what they call the longest day of the year. That's not until next June, a long time away."

Georgia sighed. "Hope we'll be out of here by then."

"Me too; it's always around my birthday." He paused. "There are races and stuff."

"For your birthday?"

"No, just part of the longest-day celebrations. But I have always won the race in my age division for the last few years. Juan was always there cheering for me." He paused for almost a minute. "Do you think we'll find him, Miss Georgia?"

Georgia reached out and took his hand. "I'm not sure what that means anymore . . . finding him."

Pablo's eyes filled with tears. "Me neither."

They were quiet for a long time, perhaps a quarter of an hour.

"We might not find him, Miss Georgia, but he will find us."

It was at this moment that Georgia realized the real meaning of what Pablo had just said. Juan Nez was dead. But his spirit was drawing them closer and closer to him. It was a light they were seeking and had begun to find. Yes, that sliver of light that could cut through the center of the spiral. That was the sign that they were drawing near the everlasting essence of Juan Nez.

She looked at the sun dagger etched in the stone again and traced it lightly with her finger.

"Pablo, this is from very long ago, right?"

"Right, Miss Georgia. Very old."

"Do you feel that we are perhaps in a very ancient part of this—what should I call it—tunnel? These rocks are so ancient. And so is this picture in the stone."

"Yes, I guess so."

"So, this could be sacred land, maybe?"

"Maybe, I don't know . . ." He paused. "I'm not old enough to know. When I come of age and have my sweat ceremony, it will be on sacred land in a special kiva. But I don't know where. They keep that stuff secret."

Georgia now began to wrestle with her own thoughts. Should she tell him about the artifacts that bore inscriptions similar to those of the sun dagger?

She began the story slowly. When she finished, Pablo looked at her.

"Why would they do that—white people do that? They might have gone into a kiva where I am not even allowed because I am too young. But I am of the land. I am Navajo. I am Diné. I would be allowed even before they would be. So why would they go? Those places are ancient and sacred. Why?"

"Money," Georgia replied.

"Then they are thieves," Pablo said softly.

"Thieves of time," Georgia whispered.

They continued walking in silence.

The pair looked constantly for cracks in the long tunnel, as it was the only way they could keep track of time. Light was becoming their guide. But whichever god controlled the light was being stingy with it. At times the tunnel widened but never to allow anything but the smallest sliver of light. *That god was a miser*, Georgia thought, *and did not dole it out in great quantities*. A sliver here, a sliver there, interspersed with long passages of darkness. But there were so many gods of light. Georgia recalled a mythology book she had as a child in Sun Prairie, Wisconsin. It was called *Servants of Light*. There was Apollo, who did double duty as the god of sun and light and poetry. Then there was Theia, known for providing the gift of sight to mankind. It was believed that the beams of light from her eyes allowed others to see. And of course, Aether was the primordial god of light and the heavenly ether.

"So where are you, folks? You so called gods," Georgia muttered. "Get on with it, already."

"Miss Georgia, I think you're talking to yourself," Pablo said.

"Oh dear, I sometimes do that, Pablo."

"That's OK, Miss Georgia. I'd rather be here with you and

not alone. So, you can keep on talking, even if it is just to yourself."

"Did I mention the Norse god of light?"

"No, what's Norse?"

"It's what they call the people in Norway. "I'll show you sometime if you come to my house. I have a globe there."

"What's a globe?"

Oh my God, thought Georgia. *The child has never seen a globe.*

"Well, Pablo, it's like a round map of the world. It's shaped like a ball. It shows all the countries, and the oceans and the continents."

"I know what a continent is," Pablo said. "A big old chunk of land. We live on a continent."

"You know which one?"

"Yep, the continent of America."

"North America, to be exact."

"If you say so." Pablo yawned.

"I say so, but you know what, Pablo?"

"What?"

"When we get out of here, I'm going to invite you to my house, and I'll show you my globe. It's a promise."

"Oh . . . oh!" he said sleepily and yawned. "I'll love that."

They spent that first night curled up against each other with just the smallest splinter of moonlight that fell through, a slit in the rock that scraped their faces. They awoke to a light that Georgia could only think of as purgatorial gray. *We're not condemned to punishment*, she thought, *but denied joy*. She looked at Pablo, who was still sleeping. What a beautiful boy he was. His long eyelashes cast spikey shadows across his face. Thank God for that. Even in this gray place, the arc of his curving cheek was lovely. If one looked hard enough one could still find beauty. God didn't make all the rules. In fact, maybe this perplexing God had challenged her to break those rules. How could one believe in God in a world of poverty and often murder and—yes—exploding appendices.

They tried to keep track of time, but they soon lost count. It was a cat-and-mouse game with the light, which was facetiously intermittent as they wound their way upward again, despite frequent but brief descents.

They were tired and hungry, but they talked—not constantly, but their conversation seeped through the long silences much like the light that trickled through the rock.

"Have you ever been stung by a bee, Miss Georgia?"

"Oh yes, couple of times at least."

"Did you stay around and watch them die?"

"Why would I do that?"

"I don't know . . . revenge? I mean, they hurt you."

"But I didn't die." They were quiet for a while. "And besides, Pablo."

"Besides what?"

"I'm back to the bee again."

"Yeah . . . what?"

"You know when a bee stings you. It loses its stinger. At least honey bees do."

"How come?"

"The stinger stays in the person when it punctures human skin."

"Can't the bee yank it out?" Pablo asked.

"Nope. It's structured in such a way it won't come out. If the bee tries, it self-amputates."

"What's 'amputate'?"

"You know. It means cutting off a limb. Like in the olden days when kings would order someone's head cut off. 'Off with their head!' a king might shout. Well, this time it's the stinger. It gets stuck in the person the bee stung. If it tries to pull out the stinger, it ruptures its stomach, and instead pulls out a string of guts—muscles, glands and a venom sac. Very gruesome death for a honey bee."

"Bluuh." Pablo let loose with a sound of revulsion. "How'd you learn all that stuff about honey bees and stingers?"

"My brothers. I think it was my brother Francis who told me about honey bees." She paused. "I learned a lot from my brothers and sisters."

"Yeah, I guess so," Pablo said in a small voice.

Georgia felt a twinge deep inside her.

"You have sisters? Brothers?"

"Nope."

A curtain had just dropped on this conversation.

Georgia recalled that St. Ambrose was the patron saint of honey bees. But who was the patron saint for her and Pablo? Who was the patron saint of sinkholes?

Pablo suddenly became very excited. Like a cat, he scaled up the tunnel wall five feet or so. Bracing himself with a foot on each of the facing tunnel walls, he called down.

"I think I can open this one more."

"Open what more?"

"The opening. The hole that lets the light through."

"How?"

"My knife."

"You have a knife with you?"

"Yeah—boy scout knife."

"You were a boy scout?"

"Yeah, the knife was the only reason I joined—and the snacks."

There was light, but Pablo could not work his knife enough to reveal more than the smallest splinter of it. There was not much to see except traces of light and more rock. Nothing appeared to offer a possible escape. It was as if they had entered a stone maze. They lost their sense of time. They found more openings but none large enough to climb through. The path they were on continued to spiral up. Sometimes near the holes the rock walls turned damp, and if Pablo dug with his knife near the base of the damp rock formations, he would find trickles of water. They had been judicious in drinking from their canteens and still had nearly half their water left. Now they both leaned against one of these damp walls. They were down to their last Tootsie Roll.

"Should we?" Pablo said, looking at the candy.

"You should. You're a growing boy."

"No, I won't eat it unless you do too."

"Oh, come on, Pablo."

"You're a growing girl." He smiled.

"Ha!" Georgia laughed harshly. A small rock suddenly

dislodged from the tunnel wall and narrowly missed Georgia's head. Like manna from heaven, light rained down on them. They looked at each other, stunned.

"Oh, my lord." Georgia seemed to exhale the words rather than speak them.

They began to climb toward the light.

TWENTY-SEVEN

Wide boards spanned the huge sinkhole and were anchored onto solid ground as firefighters wearing harnesses lowered ropes into the vast opening. One of the men on the boards was not a firefighter but a tall rangy young man with reddish hair. He had high cheekbones with an aquiline nose and the slightly sloping eyes of a Navajo. He was carrying something that looked like a small radio in one hand, and connected to the radio was an antenna. Standing next to him was Sheriff Ryan McCaffrey.

"That thing is going to buzz, right, if it detects them?" Ryan asked.

"If it detects a temperature variation," Jessie Yazzie replied. "It's a thermal differentiation detector."

"That's what you do at Stanford?"

"Some of what I do."

Jessie hoped that the sheriff didn't pry too much, for some of what he did in his junior year at Stanford was secret and now he was also, during summer break, working at Berkeley with a somewhat strange man, Robert Oppenheimer, a physicist. Jessie was working mostly on atomic orbital wave functions, but had digressed into thermal dynamics, a branch of physics that focuses on wave functions' relationship to heat temperature, energy and entropy.

He explained that the little device in his hand might be able to detect evidence of anomalous temperature variations in a sinkhole—or more precisely, to find Georgia and the young boy who had been with her. But this was a long shot, Jessie had warned the sheriff.

Georgia was the closest Jessie had to a grandmother—or mother for that matter. They had met a few years before in Taos, where he had been a part-time bartender at Los Gallos, Mabel Dodge Luhan's guest house. Mabel and Georgia both knew he was exceptionally bright and had financed his college education.

He couldn't believe it when Sheriff McCaffrey called him and told him that Georgia was missing in the Bisti Badlands and was with a young boy. He had borrowed a car and driven out as fast as he could.

"I don't want any of this to get out, Jessie. I don't want the press flocking here reporting that Georgia O'Keeffe is missing and presumed . . ." He broke off the sentence. "Well, you know what I mean."

"Yes, sir."

But Jessie wasn't actually so sure what he meant. Did he really mean the press? Or did he mean Georgia's family and her husband, Alfred Stieglitz? None of them knew about the relationship between Georgia and the sheriff. Out here, Jessie knew about their relationship, and so did Mabel Dodge Luhan and a few other people. But it was not something for public consumption. Most likely it was because Georgia wouldn't like it. She was one of the most private people he had ever met, especially for one so celebrated. So it was only a handful of Georgia's closest friends in New Mexico who knew about her relationship with Ryan.

"I wonder how long they can last beneath all that . . . that . . ." Ryan's voice dropped off again.

"Not sure, sir. But the one possibility I can think of is if this sinkhole is somehow related to a cenote, which seems kind of unlikely."

"What's a cenote?"

"It's sort of like a natural pit formed by the dissolution of rock that can result from a previous sinkhole. I think there's a lot of limestone around here and it can happen when there is a breaking up of limestone. You know those eggs over yonder."

"Eggs? What eggs?"

"Not real eggs, but egg-shaped rocks. They call them the cracked eggs. And they're mostly made out of dark limestone. That's the only visible limestone around here. But there could be more."

"What could happen then, if there were more?" Ryan asked.

"Well, it means that there could be a cenote with water and . . ."

"And they would have been either smothered to death or drowned?" Ryan inhaled sharply. "Not exactly a bright picture."

"Don't give up, Sheriff," Jessie said.

Ryan looked at the mechanical beast the county had brought in. At best it resembled a cross between an excavator and a dinosaur. The dipper on the end of the boom had three enormous teeth for digging into the sinkhole. It was too easy to imagine Georgia's limp body dangling between those teeth. And then of course there was the little boy, Pablo. Ryan had ordered a shutdown on all information about this disaster. The last thing the sheriff wanted was headlines spreading across the country that America's foremost painter had been lost in the New Mexico desert. For the first time ever, he felt a surge of compassion for Alfred Stieglitz. Georgia had never spoken ill of her husband, despite his infidelities. He had launched her career, supported her in a way that he, Ryan, never could. Through his gallery and his connections in the art world, he had made her into one of America's most popular painters. Picasso had even wanted to meet her. And so did Picasso's agent, Paul Rosenberg. But Ryan dreaded having to make the phone call to Stieglitz.

She's not dead. She can't be dead. His hands closed in tight fists. He was willing her to live.

At that moment, the device that Jessie carried beeped.

"It's found something! Something in the . . . not rock."

Ryan grabbed Jessie's shoulder. "Oh God," he muttered. Jessie began waving his arms, giving a signal to the backhoe operator to halt.

"Get over here!" Jessie called out. "I got a signal. Come quick."

The man operating the backhoe raised the bucket into the air, dismounted the machine and began racing toward Jessie. Within a minute he was standing on the board next to him.

Jessie was now holding two devices in his hands that were connected through wires.

"OK, this blinking light means a temperature differentiation has been detected. And this in my left hand, well, think of it as a compass, but they call it an interferometer. It registers interference waves, usually light or radio waves. We got one here."

"And what does that mean?" the backhoe operator asked.

"Not just rock or sand." Jessie slid his eyes toward the sheriff. "Or not alive but only recently dead. It could be a living thing or . . ." He hesitated.

"Dead."

"Dead recently. Bodies can hold a temperature, especially out here. I . . . I . . ." Jessie looked at Ryan again. "I mean, it manifests as a different kind of wave."

"Want me to use a riddle bucket?" the operator asked.

"Yes, Will. Use the riddle bucket please."

"What's that?" Ryan asked.

"Vertical tines with blunt tips."

Blunt tips. The two words screeched like a siren in Ryan's mind. Images of mangled, chopped-up bodies rising against this flawless blue sky, dripping blood, flooded his mind.

It took less than five minutes to switch to the blunt-tipped excavator bucket.

"Come off the board, Sheriff. I don't want you falling in." Jessie took him by the elbow.

"No, I'll stay right here. And don't call me Sheriff. No one knows what I am."

"Huh? You sure, sir?"

"Yes, I'm sure."

"OK, sir. Then make yourself useful. So, you hold Mabel."

Mabel was the walkie-talkie that had been very recently invented. Mabel Dodge Luhan had of course bought and donated them to police and fire departments throughout New Mexico.

For about a minute and a half, the line between the backhoe operator and Jessie crackled.

"You say, west about two degrees, at one o'clock?" Will asked.

"Yes, sir."

"But that's out of the perimeter of the sinkhole—not by much, but out of it."

"Doesn't matter," Jessie replied.

"OK."

Ryan felt his stomach knot as he watched the claws of the bucket dig into the pit. What would the blunt tines pull out? If Georgia was dead, would she be stiff by now? Generally, for at least three hours after death, a body remained flaccid and warm. A body would lose about 1.5 degrees per hour, but out here, in the summer, perhaps it's longer, as a veritable cascade of cellular death begins, beginning with the brain cells. Not long after that the body would begin to stiffen. He shut his eyes. If he opened them, would he see his dear Georgia dangling from the tines and rigid in death?

He heard Jessie catch his breath. He shut his eyes tighter. When he opened them again, Jessie was jutting his head forward as if trying to make out exactly what he was seeing suspended from the tines of the riddle bucket. It was an odd geometry of limbs, jangled appendages against the flawless blue sky.

"What the hell?" Jessie gasped. "A donkey?"

Slowly and delicately, Will swung the bucket until it was over the ground and set it down as if lowering a sleeping baby into a crib.

"A donkey, just a donkey?" Ryan croaked. He felt as though he was teetering on the edge of manic laughter.

The walkie-talkies crackled again. "Hold on, folks, I'm going back for another scoop. There's something else down there . . ."

"No!" Ryan choked.

TWENTY-EIGHT

Pablo was scrambling up toward the light.

"Ditłéé'," he gasped.

"Ditłéé'? What's that?" Georgia asked.

"Wet. We're near water," he called down—he was at least ten feet above her. "Water's better than Tootsie Rolls."

They began to climb toward the light, scratching and groping their way up the wall, which luckily was at a gentle angle. The passageway began to open up more. They felt they must be moving toward some sort of way out, when Pablo blurted a string of words in Navajo that Georgia didn't understand. He stopped abruptly. Turning around, his face was pale. A light of fear danced in his eyes.

"I don't think we should be here." He paused. His lips were trembling. "It's . . . it's the place of the dead. The cliffs."

"Oh," Georgia replied softly. She recalled the funeral procession that she had watched from afar with David McAlpin as the people from Far Cry had carried the bodies of Edgar Adahki and his wife, Alice, wrapped in canvas on boards up to the cliffs.

"No, I guess we shouldn't, but where should we go?"

"There might be a lead off from here somewhere," Pablo said.

"A lead? What do you mean?"

"Another way to get to those cliffs over there, farther from these. Not good for living people to visit the dead."

At that moment, as if to reinforce what Pablo had just said, a shadow obliterated the light as the vast wingspan of a vulture flew overhead. There was a sudden raspy, hissing sound as the shadow vanished, and then they saw the vulture diving toward a tree.

"He's going to tear at the wrapping on the board if there is one in that tree. We have to get out of here," Pablo said.

"This is bad. We are too close to the dead. The skinwalkers will catch us . . . and . . . and feed us to the vultures."

Georgia remembered what Lucille had said about the heavy-duty canvas that could resist the attacks of buzzards on bodies.

There were a thousand things that Georgia wanted to say to calm Pablo. But who was she? Just an old white lady who most likely didn't believe in their superstitions. And what did she know? Absolutely nothing about their spiritual beliefs. And, even more important, what did she believe in? She just knew one thing: that all religions, as she had once said in an interview, were human made. And even though she had been born a Catholic, she was not "in" a religion. Nevertheless, she felt in one sense very religious. Having religion for Georgia meant having respect for other people and their beliefs. Not necessarily following those beliefs herself, but simply recognizing that other people might believe differently. And she held a deep respect for Pablo and was in constant awe of the life around her. By "life", she meant earth and sky and everything that inspired her to paint.

She reached out her hand and clasped Pablo's. "Yes, Pablo, let's find another way out of here . . . there must be one."

And so, they continued. The tunnel went on and on through the cliffs. The splinters of sunlight that guided them for several hours of the day soon vanished and were swallowed by the twilight lavender of the coming evening. They consumed their last Tootsie Roll, and they found enough trickles of water to quench their parched throats without having to use their canteens. It tasted a bit gritty, but it was wet.

Was there another way out? They were unsure. When they did occasionally emerge, the cliffs were so precipitous that trying to descend them would be treacherous, especially since the wind had picked up and was blowing fiercely. Georgia felt as though they were in an endless maze, but this was preferable to being buried under who knew how many tons of sand. There had to be a way out . . . a way down . . . or up? Every time they were able to stick their heads out of a narrow gap in the cliff walls, it was a sheer drop of at least five hundred feet.

"If only we had wings." Pablo sighed.

"How long has it been, Pablo?" Georgia asked.

"I don't know." He paused. "But I feel that we are farther and farther away from Juan. Don't you?" His voice cracked.

She was uncertain how to answer. If she said "yes", that would confirm that they were losing hope. Then she wondered suddenly if people were losing hope about them? Surely Orville and Ansel must be worried. And what would Ryan think if she never returned? What would Stieglitz think? She couldn't bear the idea of never seeing either of them again.

"Miss Georgia, are you crying?"

"No . . . well, maybe yes." She grasped Pablo's hand.

And the question that they were both wondering hung in the air unspoken. *Are we going to die?*

TWENTY-NINE

The riddle bucket was silhouetted against the setting sun. Something was dangling between the blunt teeth of the bucket, and it was not a donkey. And yet, it seemed to be incomplete somehow.

"What is that?" Jessie whispered. "I see arms." He paused. "No, just one arm."

Ryan's eyes were shut tight. He could not bear to look. "Is it her, Jessie? Is it Georgia?" He choked.

"No . . . no . . . it's a man." He felt Ryan waver. "Steady there, sir. It's not Georgia."

"Es un hombre!" someone yelled as the silhouette of the bucket with the dangling body printed against the setting sun. The figure appeared as if caught in some manic dance.

"Es Juan Nez. Es el Hombre Burro."

"Donkey Man!" someone shouted.

Ryan registered that name as belonging to Juan Nez, Georgia's bone man. How had this come about? Did that mean that Georgia was nearby? Georgia and the little boy, Pablo?

"Let's go down, Sheriff," Jessie said.

A tall gentleman began to walk out on the plank.

"Step back, sir. Off the plank," a fireman ordered.

"But, sir, I am the head of the archaeology expedition, and I know the strata, the rocks, the geology inside out."

"It's a safety issue, sir. I'll talk to you off the plank and be happy to listen to you. But for now, stand aside, and I'll be with you in a minute."

Ryan winced as he heard Douglas Acheson speaking.

"You know as an archaeologist I am very familiar with the geological strata out here . . ." The guy wouldn't give up. Why did some people need to assert themselves this way? What were they trying to prove? Acheson walked off the plank and stood next to another younger man.

This was why Ryan was out here, of course. To investigate the very archaeology site the man had mentioned. Which he didn't give a crap about now. All he could think about was Georgia smothering to death, or perhaps drowning, if Jessie's cenote theory was true. Was there another body that the bucket was going to pull up? Had Georgia been with Juan? She was so fond of the old guy. He had a nose for bones, as she put it.

People had crowded close to where the riddle bucket had deposited the body of Juan Nez.

"Stand back, folks. Stand back." Joe Descheeni was directing people to make room. He arrived soon after they talked on the radio. Ryan caught his eye and gave a barely discernible shake of his head, which Joe immediately read as *don't blow my cover*.

"Dr. Watson." Joe turned to Ryan. "I know you're a dentist and not a coroner."

"True, true indeed."

"But since you're the closest person here with a medical background, do you see anything that should be noted?"

"Well, yes, sir. It's pretty obvious. This man's arm was practically severed at the shoulder. I don't know if sinkholes can tear a person apart like that. It seems sort of odd. Or maybe I should say incongruous. Suffocation, yes, but a severed arm? I don't know. I'm sorry, but I think that's all I can answer at the moment. A coroner could tell you better. I'm just a retired dentist."

"Yeah, I was thinking the same thing myself and I'm not even a dentist," Joe replied.

A siren sounded. "OK, folks, step back. Got an ambulance coming in from Farmington."

Two men stepped out from the ambulance and went to the rear to unload a stretcher.

"You got a second stretcher?" Joe asked.

"Two?" one man asked.

"We got a dead donkey here."

"No, we only have one."

"Take them together. One on top of the other," Ryan barked.

"The doctor says take them both," Joe said.

Instant respect! Ryan marveled. *Maybe I should have been a dentist instead of a cop*, he thought. But Georgia had told him how close Juan was to his donkey and the load of bones the creature had carried for her.

And so, they loaded the donkey first and then placed the old man, Juan Nez, on top.

"Careful with that arm of his," Ryan directed. "Those deltoid muscles are pretty much shredded from the look of things." There! He had rendered a medical opinion. He felt somewhat vindicated in his fraudulent profession.

THIRTY

As Ryan McCaffrey turned and walked back toward his car, he saw Tommy Tso, whom he had met at Hosteen Tsinajine's hogan, was waiting for him with the girl Wynnie Haloke.

"We got another problem," Tommy said gravely.

"Worse than this one?"

"Maybe about the same."

"What is it?"

"Another dead body."

The color drained from Ryan's face.

"Who?"

"A woman. Regina Phelps, the lady who underwrites the entire archaeology dig."

"Where did they find her?"

"On a gas well road about ten miles outside of Farmington. The body was dragged into a culvert. A gas well monitor found her." He took a big inhale. "But here's what's interesting."

"Yeah? What's that?"

"Lucille Samuels, who runs the trading post, had called for Regina Phelps' usual driver. He was running late. She had been waiting for him in the barn. Lucille checked on her because the driver was late, but she was gone. Just vanished. Like that." Tommy snapped his fingers. "Lucille said that she saw Mrs. Phelps having a yelling match with a young woman before she asked for the driver to pick her up—from her description of that woman, I'm assuming it's her stepdaughter, Marya Phelps."

Wynnie made a face at the mention of Marya.

Ryan recalled now that the trading post woman had at first thought he was the driver who was to take a woman to Farmington. But he didn't know about the fight.

"Gone, yes?"

"Now dead."

"And she was underwriting this whole excavation, you say?" Ryan asked.

"Yep, and she had been underwriting it for the last three years."

"OK, I don't want anybody here to know about her disappearance, or her death."

"Whatever you say, Sheriff."

Ryan winced and stepped closer to Tommy. "And don't, for God's sake, call me Sheriff. No one here knows except Orville, and Jessie over there, out on the plank, and Joe Descheeni, my deputy from Santa Fe."

"Who's Jessie?" Tommy asked.

"Smartest guy in New Mexico and close friend of Georgia O'Keeffe."

Wynnie walked up looking very grim. "Pablo Jemez was with Georgia," she said softly.

"Oh shit!" Tommy blurted out. "That's my cousin!" He turned to Wynnie. "Are you sure they were together?"

"Yes, that's what Orville said."

"They . . . they could have been swallowed up . . . like Juan Nez and his donkey." Ryan pinched the bridge of his nose as if he were forcing back an image.

"Juan was swallowed?" Tommy blurted. "He's been missing I think for close to three weeks now. Everyone was out looking for him and his donkey."

"You say close to three weeks he's been missing?" Ryan asked.

"Yes, sir."

"Three weeks ago, there was no sinkhole here. So, he couldn't have died in it." Ryan inhaled deeply. "He must have died before the sinkhole occurred." The image of the nearly severed arm flashed in his mind.

"You never can tell, sir," Jessie said, walking up to them and gripping Ryan's shoulder.

"Tell what? What do you mean, Jessie?"

"I mean, remember how Juan's body was found just outside of the perimeter of the funnel of the sinkhole? The Bisti Badlands are full of surprises—slot canyons, cenotes—it's a tangled terrain beneath all this. Canyons within canyons. Cliffs with tongues."

"Tongues?"

"You know, shafts, and all sorts of water sources, if they're lucky and alert. It's another world down there, another universe."

Ryan took a deep breath, then shook his head. "Honestly, Jessie, don't take this the wrong way, but I think when you say that the Bisti Badlands has lots of tongues and surprises, well the surprise here is murder. Juan Nez must have been murdered. And maybe the murderer tried to bury him and the donkey out here, and the grave was swallowed by the sinkhole. A hole in a hole."

Ansel Adams was now approaching. "Orville is sure this was where Georgia had last been painting." He paused and looked about. "According to Orville, she had become obsessed with this place because there was a slot canyon near here." He paused. "But it might have been because of that rack of antlers right over there as well."

"Betcha anything those are the antlers that Juan found for her," Ryan said. "She'd written to me about them just a few days ago. She was . . . was . . ." His voice broke. "So excited to have found them."

He looked around. Orville was heading toward them now. The last thing he wanted was him shouting out, "Howdy, Sheriff". So, he hurried over to him and grasped his hand. "For purposes right now, nobody here knows me as Sheriff, please. I'm a dentist."

Orville blinked. "You don't say! Well, it was the antlers that drew Georgia here. Put a frame around them and tell me that is not a Georgia O'Keeffe painting come to life."

To life! The words echoed in Ryan's brain.

"Look, Orville, I can't explain it all," he said, "But I actually came out here on another matter. Didn't know about this sinkhole disaster until I got here."

"Another matter?" Orville asked.

"Yeah, I can't discuss it here." He nodded toward the cluster of the archaeology team that had gathered.

"All right, sir." He looked straight at the left-hand side of Ryan's shirt where he usually wore the sheriff's star. Ryan caught his glance.

"I'm an amateur astronomer now—and a retired dentist, come out to see the Pleiades. Don't ask me too much. What I know about stars is precious little. And less about dentistry."

Douglas Acheson was now striding toward them, accompanied by another man.

"No progress, I gather, Mr. . . ." Acheson paused. "I don't believe I caught your name before."

"Watson," Ryan said. "Jim Watson." At least he remembered that he had never given himself a fake name when he told him about his fake leisure pursuit of stargazing. "I don't think I ever introduced myself," Ryan said.

"And this is my chief field assistant, Gideon Blake," Acheson replied.

"Pleased to meet you, Mr. Blake." Ryan extended his hand. He noticed some scratches on his right cheek and jaw. "Looks like you had a tangle with a prickly pear."

"Oh yeah. Took a tumble from my horse and landed in the wrong place." He raised his hand to his jaw. His nails were short, bitten down to the quick.

"So, how is your dig going?" Ryan asked.

"Excellently," Acheson said. "We've found some extraordinary artifacts that predate anything that's been found out here before."

"Before Chaco," Orville chimed in. "Or so they say." He slid his eyes toward Acheson.

"Absolutely." Acheson nodded enthusiastically.

"That must please Mrs. Phelps," Orville offered.

"Oh yes!" Acheson and Blake exclaimed simultaneously.

"She's thrilled," Acheson said.

"Now, who's Mrs. Phelps?" Ryan asked innocently.

Orville picked it up immediately. "Rich lady from back east, friend of the archaeologists out here. Supports many digs. Archaeology is her passion."

"Is she out here now?" Ryan asked.

"No," Acheson said. "She had to go back to Far Cry. She

was going to meet her stepdaughter. I drove her there myself. I think Regina said something about Marya wanting to borrow money from her. That girl is always on her tail because Regina inherited most of the fortune of her late husband, the stepdaughter's father. As far as I know, Marya has enough to get by, but she seems greedy. I'm sure Regina will be back soon though," he said brightly.

Ryan was regarding the two men from Yale carefully. He was in a delicate position. He knew something that these two men at least seemed to know nothing about: that Regina Phelps' body had been found. It was in a strange way a relief, as his eyes rested upon the teeth of the bucket that was hanging off the end of the boom. No more bodies dragged up so far. Yet in a culvert near a gas rig, a body had been found—the body of one Regina Phelps. And where was this stepdaughter of hers now?

"How do you account for her interest in archaeology?" Ryan asked, bringing the conversation back to the questionable dig. "Kind of like mine in astronomy?" He turned to Ansel and Orville. "I'm an amateur astronomer. That's why I came out here. Good time to view the Pleiades."

"Oh yeah," Ansel said, not too convincingly.

Acheson inhaled deeply. He was settling into the professorial posture that was familiar to him. The words began to flow as if he were in a classroom lecturing. "Well, you see, Mr. Watson." The name sounded ridiculous to Ryan's ears. Why had he chosen the name Watson? As in Sherlock and Watson? He had to get better at this. Acheson continued. He appeared to like an audience, even a small one. "Archaeology is nothing more," he paused, "or less, than stories. We all love stories, don't we? And so does Regina Phelps. She is passionate about the stories archaeology can tell."

Ryan could see that Professor Acheson was in his element now. This was most likely his opening lecture in Archaeology 101. "It's the story of earth and humankind through the reconstruction of the material remains from their cultures. When and how we became what we are. The detritus, so to speak; things that are left behind. Ultimately, perhaps, as Ruth Benedict has said, 'To make the world safe for human differences.' So, in one sense I'm a finder but I am also a listener . . . I listen to the stories that the strata reveal and attempt to interpret them." He paused, almost as if waiting for applause. Ryan did not applaud.

What a fabulist this fellow is, Ryan thought. Handsome speech. Mostly true, but wasn't it a cover for something else? Ryan had a knack for piercing through cover stories. He had just created one about himself, after all: Watson, retired dentist and amateur astronomer, just to put the cherry on the ice-cream sundae. He'd listened to too many liars over the years—liars, murderers, cheats, and crooks. And soon it would be time to dig into this stratum of verbiage that Professor Acheson had just dumped on him. Well, not yet. Douglas Acheson, the professor of Archaeology at Yale, was on a roll.

"Take you for example, sir," Acheson resumed and looked directly at Ryan. "You point your telescope to the skies, the stars, and can possibly glimpse the beginnings of the universe. Or so Einstein suggests."

"He does?" Ryan said. "I just remembered a quote I read that Einstein said about the universe, something about how he was uncertain if the universe was infinite but that people's stupidity is definitely limitless."

"God, what a great quote!" Blake slapped his knee.

He should credit Georgia for that one. For some reason she had an endless supply of Einstein quotes. She could trot them out at just the right moment. Suddenly it was as if a tidal wave of grief rose within him. He looked into the distance and sighed deeply. Then, closing his eyes, Ryan—or rather Dr. Watson—murmured, seemingly to himself, "No, I don't look for anything as grand as the beginnings of the universe. I look at the stars just for stories. Stories have beginnings and endings." Then opening his eyes, he went on abruptly: "What do you think about this artist who may have been swallowed in the sinkhole?"

"Georgia O'Keeffe?" Acheson sighed. "I don't know. It doesn't look promising."

"No, it doesn't," Blake said. "She came to our camp once

or twice. It was when we were celebrating a new find. She seemed really nice."

"What find were you celebrating?"

"Some pottery fragments that showed—at least, we think—the rainbow arc, a spiraling design. But these were pre-Chaco Canyon, which means pre-850 years, common era."

"So that's a big deal?" Ryan asked.

"I'll say!" Blake exclaimed.

Acheson took a step closer and fixed Ryan with a stare, then lowered his voice. "It's possibly the biggest deal in American archaeology this century."

"Well, good luck to you."

"And what do you do when you don't amateur stargaze?" Acheson asked.

"I'm a retired dentist."

"Dentist?"

"No kidding?" Blake said.

"From dentistry to stargazing, wow!" Acheson marveled.

"Different view," Ryan replied. "Finite versus infinity."

"Guess so." Blake chuckled.

"No time to wonder when you're looking in somebody's mouth, doing say a root canal," Acheson said.

"I had a lousy one done before I came out here," Blake interjected. "The crown is coming loose already, I think. You want to take a look at it?"

"No. Don't have the right tools anyway." Ryan paused. How far was he going to try running with this? He could have said he was a retired plumber. At least he hadn't said he was an astrophysicist, just an innocent stargazer.

"The right tools?" Blake asked.

"You know—drill, bur. Best in the business are the Webster endodontic burs." Ryan's late wife Mattie's brother was a dentist, so he'd picked up some of the lingo from him. Just enough to sprinkle a few impressive-sounding words into this little discourse.

"I see you moved your jeep over here, Dr. Watson," Acheson said. Ryan blinked. He was certainly not accustomed to being addressed as a doctor.

"Well, I thought if they needed more vehicles or someone to run to Farmington, I might be helpful."

"And your skills as a doctor if they bring them out alive."

"Just a dentist. Not sure if my training would apply in this situation."

"What do you think their chances are for survival?" Acheson asked.

"No idea," Ryan replied wearily.

"Sad." Acheson shook his head. "We'd better be heading back to our camp. We got a lot of packing up to do as we leave soon. We have to, you know, secure the site, and all that."

"Sure thing," Ryan replied.

The three men shook hands and Ryan watched as they headed toward their horses, mounted them and disappeared into the dusk. They were turning north and slightly west, which was not the direction of the camp at all. Did they have to go to Far Cry first?

THIRTY-ONE

Pablo was worried. Georgia was moving more and more slowly, and she was breathing heavily. It was becoming harder to tell the time as the tunnel cracks had seemed to be farther in between, affording few glimpses of the outside world. And those openings had become narrower and narrower. "Like looking through the eye of a needle," Georgia had said. For perhaps the tenth time this day, whatever day this was, she had to stop and rest.

He looked at her now, propped against the rock wall, dozing. Her face seemed to resemble rock. The wrinkles had become deeper. He had never thought of her as being old before. But now she looked really old. Her face was thinner, and her body looked so frail. It was like one of the stick figures in the rock carvings. He suddenly thought of the humpback flute player Kokopelli. Put a flute in Georgia's mouth and some feathers in her hair and she would be Kokopelli, even without the humped back. Pablo smiled at that.

"What's so funny?" she growled.

"You look like Kokopelli."

"What?"

"Kokopelli, the humpback flute-playing god."

"Oh, thanks. Not Greta Garbo?"

"Who's Greta Garbo?"

"Never mind."

"Kokopelli brings good luck."

"Well, where is she now? We need some luck," Georgia whispered hoarsely, shut her eyes, and was soon fast asleep. What did she dream about, Pablo wondered. Colors, shapes, bones—all those bones Juan found for her. Why did she love bones so much? Bones mean death. Did she see life in death? Or beauty in death?

At that moment a breeze seemed to stir the air. Pablo felt

something. A presence. He glanced toward Georgia, who now looked like a broken scarecrow propped against the stone wall. Did she feel that breeze too, the presence? No, she was sound asleep and snoring lightly. But Pablo felt it. He was here. Juan was here!

Pablo got up and walked a short distance down the tunnel. The path began to curve sharply. The color of the rock walls shifted from rust to a pale gray. He was entering a different region. Was he just imagining it, or had the spirit of Juan become stronger?

The tunnel suddenly widened and began to climb steeply. He was just about to take another step when something caught his eye that seemed alien. He crouched down and saw that it was a cigarette butt, smoked down to a quarter of an inch. Odd place to be smoking. It couldn't have just blown here. He scanned this stretch of the path and spotted a gap in the ceiling ahead. He hurried toward it. Then, standing up to his full height, he put one foot on a protruding rock and hoisted himself up a bit. Bracing himself, he looked for another foothold. It was a stretch, but he found one. Then another, and then another. Finally, he was at the rim and found himself peering into a large, cavernous space.

"Yáadilá óolyé," he swore softly to himself. His eyes opened wide as he took in the extraordinary site. He felt as though he was teetering on the brink of legend. This was a sipapu, the ancient portal through which the first creatures emerged into the world, sloughing off their lizard forms and became human.

First People! I am living the legend!

THIRTY-TWO

The crowds of onlookers at the site had thinned. Only the rescuers were left. Tommy and Wynnie were still with Ryan. Ryan quickly set up his telescope on the roof of his jeep, then, crouching on his knees, he began to track Professor Acheson and his assistant as they headed in a direction that was not in the vicinity of their archaeology site. They took a sharp left but at that point he lost them.

"What the devil are they doing?" he murmured to himself.

The view was now blotted out as a familiar figure walked into his sights.

"Goddammit!" he muttered. It was Joe Descheeni.

His deputy looked up at him. "Hey there. Stargazing, I guess."

Ryan looked down at him from the roof of the Willys jeep. "Sort of. What is it?"

"They came up with something more on the murder outside of Farmington," Joe replied. Tommy and Wynnie moved closer to them to hear what the news was about.

"What's that?" Ryan asked.

"The victim had traces of chloroform in her blood at high concentrations."

Wynnie gasped.

"Chloroform?" Ryan asked.

"Yep. I told the police department in Farmington not to say anything," Joe replied.

"Is Max Schaffer still the captain over there?"

"Yep."

"He's a good guy. Did you tell him I'm working on something over here?"

"I did. He says he'll stand by if you need help."

"Ok, I'll pack up my telescope and come down." He got down from the car's roof and waved at Orville to come over.

"Joe, they called you in on this?" Orville asked.

"Not exactly," Joe replied.

"We got a criminal case on our hands," Ryan spoke softly.

"What?" Orville said. "How does a sinkhole turn into a criminal case?"

"Not related," Ryan replied and quickly explained the situation.

"Mrs. Phelps murdered? And . . . and . . . you think this stepdaughter of hers might be involved? Plus, the situation with Acheson and Blake?" Orville stammered. He was clearly overwhelmed by the information.

Ryan quickly explained the suspect artifacts.

"Why does this not surprise me? Not at all. I thought they might be working on sacred land. I didn't know where." Orville now nodded toward the cliffs.

"But you think up there?" Ryan asked.

"Possibly," Orville said.

"Are those cliffs climbable?" Ryan asked.

"If you can find the right path. To the south where the juniper grows. That's where the Indian folks take their dead. They hoist them into the trees on planks. There's a trail that I think leads to those junipers and makes the cliffs fairly reachable. You don't have to be much of a mountain climber to get there."

"And what might be there at the top?"

"I'm a white guy. I don't know, but I think it's sacred land up there. You couldn't get a permit to dig without permission from the tribal council."

THIRTY-THREE

"OK, we're almost there, Miss Georgia, almost. And when we get there, I might be able to lift you up and push you through the hole."

"You think so?" Her breathing was very labored. Pablo knew if they could only get to this place, to the kiva—for that was what he was certain it was—they would find their way out.

Pablo had experienced an indescribable feeling when that golden light poured down on him as he clambered his way through the hole, the sipapu. *This is the floor of a kiva!* he thought. It was just like the story told when First People emerged into the world. This kiva was where the men went for their special ceremonies. His grandfather had told him about one, and had sworn him to secrecy, but promised that when he got old enough, he too could come to the kiva and learn the ceremonies and the chants.

He looked back at Georgia, still crumpled against the wall. Her knobby knees were sticking up. Her long bony fingers clutched her knees. Her elbows jutted out—she was no longer the flute player he thought, but Spider Woman, the killer of monsters. But this collapsed pile of bones hardly looked like a threat. Nevertheless, it was as if a stampede of mythological figures flowed through Pablo's mind. As he teetered on a brink between two worlds—that of legend and that of now—he felt he might lose his balance and tumble back into the unreal of legend. But he must go to the real world, the Fourth World. He and Miss Georgia had come through the First World, the Black World, then the Second World, the Blue World of animals. The Third World that was Yellow, the world of twilight, and finally in the Fourth World was the world of humans. But it was Spider Woman who helped the creatures from one world to the next. And then he spied through the hole a ladder leaning against the wall above. It was a kiva ladder that allowed the men from outside to descend into the kiva.

This was indeed the place his grandfather had told him about. Where he would go for his coming-of-age ceremony; where the elders would lash him with the strands from a yucca plant, and chant in this kiva which would become a sweat lodge. But there was no fire, no yucca, and yet here he was, ready to become a man and go into the Fourth World and lead Georgia with him.

"Miss Georgia!" he called out. "Miss Georgia, come and help me. Help me."

"What?" she said weakly.

"I found the place!"

"What?"

"The sacred place," he began to stammer. "And . . . and . . ."

"And what?" Georgia could barely raise her voice above a whisper.

"I think I've found a way out. There is even a ladder to help us."

"I'm not sure I can make it."

"Of course you can. I know you can." His voice cracked. "Come, Miss Georgia," he barked. He wanted to say *this is where the world began, our world*. But she wouldn't understand. For now, it was just the way out and back to where they belonged.

"I can't, Pablo. I just can't."

He scrambled back down and dropped to his knees by her side.

"You go, Pablo. You're young. I have had a long, beautiful life."

The words were meaningless to Pablo. She knew they would be, but they were the truth. What a life she had had! She recalled one of her very first memories from when she was just a toddler. It was the dirt in Sun Prairie, Wisconsin. It was bright yellow and very soft. The story was told that her mother once caught her eating it. It might have been shortly after when she tried making a picture with some finger paints that her mother had set out for her and her older brother Francis.

Swirly . . . that was a word she often used when trying to explain those early efforts. "I like to make swirly pictures," she would say. And she did, with lots of yellow and red. The sun maybe swirling through the sky with red clouds tumbling about. Who knows? Georgia chuckled.

"Miss Georgia, don't laugh. This isn't funny," Pablo begged her and shook her shoulder.

Yes, it is funny, she wanted to say, but the words wouldn't come. It's very funny. And how did she get from that swirly painting of a sun tumbling across the sky to the painting of the huge black crosses on the moradas? Oh, those crosses! She was fascinated by them—those thin dark veils of the Catholic church. But the starry nights . . . the background . . . beautiful . . . not beautiful, you say? Oppressive . . . well doggonit, that's the church for you . . . a riddle, she thought . . . No, that was Ryan who said that . . . or maybe someone else . . . *Oh, Ryan, darling, I miss you.*

"It is not beautiful if you die here," Pablo's voice cut in harshly on her musings. Georgia's eyes flew open.

"Who taught you to speak that way, young man?"

"Me! I taught myself. I've always taught myself until I met you. And you're coming with me." His eyes were dark and furious. He scooped his hands beneath her shoulder blades and dragged her into a sitting position.

"What are you doing?"

"I'm dragging you into the next world whether you like it or not," he hissed furiously.

Pablo succeeded in getting her to the ledge just beneath the hole, but she crumpled again. However, dragging was different from lifting. He would have to lift her to shove her through the sipapu. If he dropped her, she would shatter like broken pottery. All that would be left would be fragments and dust. He was breathing hard. Now he climbed over her and looked up again. The ladder! Of course, but would it fit through this hole? She could climb, would climb, if he got behind her and shoved. He would just have to stuff her into the next world.

"Stay here," he ordered.

"You think I'm going somewhere?" She gave a throaty laugh.

Good sign. She's joking, Pablo thought while climbing over her. He then scrambled out of the hole.

The ladder was narrow. It would fit through the hole and, if she could climb it, they could get out. Something caught his eye as he began to move the ladder toward the hole. Propped against the same wall as the ladder was a canteen. He stopped immediately and took it. He heard water sloshing inside. "Water! Miss Georgia, I found water—lots."

There was no answer. He put the strap of the canteen around his neck and continued to move the ladder toward the sipapu. "I'm coming, Miss Georgia. I'm coming, and I have a surprise for you. Hear that—a surprise!"

In another two minutes he had slipped the ladder through the hole and descended to where Georgia was propped against a wall and sound asleep again. He pinched her arm to waken her. "Wake up, I got water here."

"Huh?" she croaked. He unscrewed the top. "Open your mouth." He tipped the neck of the canteen just a bit toward her lips. "Do you taste that?"

"Yes," she said hoarsely. She blinked. "You're a wonder, Pablo."

"Drink some more."

"No, you should," she replied.

"No, you're older."

"That's no excuse."

Pablo sighed. "Miss Georgia, can we please not argue. I'll take some if you take another swallow. There's plenty in there."

"All right." She took several swallows. The water seemed to revive her a bit.

Pablo squatted right in front of her to speak. "Now here's what we're going to do. I'm going to prop you up against the ladder and then you take a step on it, and I'll push you up to the next step. Just hang on with your hands tight and when you're ready for me to push, say 'ready' and I'll push on your butt again. I'll be right behind you."

They began to climb the ladder. Pablo kept shoving on Georgia's butt. It felt like the skinniest butt in the world. Certainly, the boniest butt he could have ever imagined. But she was making the steps and seemed to be gathering strength.

Suddenly, she emitted a tiny shriek. "No!" she gasped. The peculiar design, the colors sorted themselves out in her brain and it became a horrifying realization. The jet-black round eyes, the colorful beaded body and now the hiss that sizzled the air as the bright-blue forked tongue shot out of the reptile's mouth.

"Pablo, it's a Gila monster!"

Unlike Cerberus, the multi-headed dog guarding the gates of hell, this creature only had one head. But there was not going to be any passage out of this hell. No transit to the Fourth World. Georgia began to sink.

"No, Miss Georgia!" Pablo screamed as she tumbled back. They both crashed together onto the ground. Looking up, they saw the creature staring back at them with its unblinking dark eyes. A ray of sunshine struck its scales. How could something look so hideous and splendid at the same time, Georgia wondered. The reptile was perched like a dazzling jewel at the gates of the world they yearned to reach.

THIRTY-FOUR

Wynnie Haloke and Tommy Tso were still at the site of the sinkhole. In the wake of this tragedy, their own problems shrunk to minuscule proportions. There was nothing like real tragedy to draw one back into conversation, even after Wynnie's discovery of Tommy's infidelity. It all felt somewhat trifling in comparison.

They walked back to the car in the quiet of the sunset, as there wasn't much for them to do there. They were still shocked about Juan's death and now they had just heard about Regina's murder.

"Why? Why would anybody do that to Mrs. Phelps?" Wynnie mused. "I can't believe it. You know when she first came, I thought she was just some stuck-up rich bitch."

"What changed your mind?" Tommy asked.

"Well, she seemed disturbed when I raised the question about the possibility of working on sacred lands. It was when I found the first potsherds that they all became so excited. She asked me about it."

"What did you say?"

"Not much." She paused. "It just surprised me, really. I realized I had thought of her as just a rich lady. You know, come out here and get her kicks from getting her hands slightly dirty groveling in the dirt. I didn't think she really saw me much as a person—or maybe just a slightly exotic person, being Navajo and all. She had a whole collection of jewelry by Kenneth Begay and Alina Chee."

Tommy gave a low whistle. "Whoa, those pieces fetch over a thousand dollars."

"Yep, she has a different one for every day." They were silent for almost a minute. "Maybe someone was trying to steal them? Maybe her stepdaughter Marya stole them to pawn them?"

"Good question," Tommy said. "I'm going to tell the cops

to check it out and see if anything shows up on the black market." He sighed.

Just as they were approaching the parked car, Wynnie stopped.

"What is it?" Tommy asked.

"Why would someone use chloroform for murder?"

"Not sure. Maybe they didn't have a gun or a knife. Just kind of a clean way—if that's the word—to kill someone. Overdose them with chloroform. It would have to be a lot of chloroform to actually kill a person, I think."

"Do they use chloroform in hospitals?"

"I think they mostly use ether, not chloroform."

"Where do they use chloroform, then?" Wynnie asked.

"Maybe veterinarians. Large animal vets."

"Hmm . . ." Wynnie said.

They were silent for a long time before they got into the car. Lucille came up and asked, "You riding with me, Wynnie?"

Then, almost casually, Wynnie replied: "No thanks, I think I'll ride back with Tommy."

Later that night in bed, sleeping next to him, Wynnie was lost in a dream that made absolutely no sense to her. It was about a farm and animals and filing horses' hooves and maybe delivering a breech birth of a cow. She would not remember it until late the following morning when the phone rang, and Tommy answered it.

"Hi, Uncle, what's up . . .? What! Strange. Did you call the police?" Wynnie looked up from the biscuits she was making for their late breakfast.

"What is it?" she mouthed.

"Hang on a second. I'll call you right back," Tommy said to his uncle and hung up the phone.

"It's my Uncle Erwin over in Kirtland. He just discovered that some containers of chloroform were stolen from him."

"What was he doing with chloroform?"

"He's a large-animal vet." He paused for just a second. "I gotta call him back."

Wynnie put her hand to her chest and gasped. Her dream

came back to her, along with some words, but not from a dream. They were words that Gideon Blake had spoken that evening after her find at the dig, as he went on about her tender fingertips which were so different to his. *Try filing a hoof on a large plow animal . . . or just digging in the dirt all day for potatoes . . . but digging for stories . . . that was my dream come true.* Farm boy turned Yale scholarship student, so he could dig with his roughened hands into the dirt—*digging for stories . . . that was my dream come true.*

"Uncle Erwin, you gotta call the cops in Farmington about this. There was a murder out here, and the cause of death was chloroform."

Tommy paused and looked at Wynnie as his uncle continued speaking.

"I'm not jumping to any conclusions, Uncle. I'm just saying it seems kind of odd, that's all." He paused now. "OK, goodbye. I'll keep you posted, and you do the same."

Tommy hung up the phone again and turned toward Wynnie.

"How about that? Some coincidence."

"How about it? And I know who did it." Wynnie was almost jumping up and down.

"What do you mean?"

"I know the murderer. I know who it is!"

Tommy shook his head in disbelief. "How?"

"Sit down and I'll tell you."

Tommy was silent for several seconds after she told him her story. "It's a big leap, Wynnie."

"Not really," she said insistently.

"Not really? Just because this guy . . . what's his name again?"

"Gideon Blake."

"Just because he grew up on a farm doesn't mean he did it. I mean, how many other kids on that dig—students—might have grown up on farms? I doubt you know all of them and their personal histories. And what about Marya? She would have a good reason to kill Regina, as far as I understand."

"Mmmm . . ." was all that Wynnie said. She turned to him

now. "At least I think you should tell Sheriff McCaffrey about this. That your uncle's chloroform supply was stolen."

"Oh, I will, definitely." He turned to her and gave her a pat on the cheek. She found the gesture a bit demeaning but decided not to say anything.

THIRTY-FIVE

Georgia leaned against the rock wall. She seemed somewhat revived after the shock of the Gila monster. "This reminds me of that game."

"What game?" Pablo asked.

"You know the . . . the game with all those properties like Park Place and Baltic Avenue. I think there was one called Ventnor Avenue."

"What are you talking about?" Pablo asked.

"Monopoly! That's the name of the game. Everyone wanted to land on Park Place. You could charge a lot of rent. Very high class, ritzy location. Not like us." She looked up and saw the Gila monster's piercing gaze. "I hope that it doesn't come down here and attack us."

"They don't attack unless they're threatened."

"Hmmm," Georgia replied. "What do we do now?"

"We wait," Pablo said.

Georgia dozed off again. She was uncertain how long she had been asleep but when she opened her eyes, the Gila monster was still there, and now Pablo was creeping up the ladder toward it. He must have sensed Georgia waking up and turned to give her a fierce look. His eyes said, "Don't you dare."

Was he really going to try Juan Nez's trick of hypnotizing the creature? A creature that was said to be much more venomous than a rattlesnake. Ten minutes passed before Georgia heard a softly resonant sound curling up from Pablo's throat. She almost gasped when she realized that Pablo's face was mere inches, no more than four, from the Gila monster. Pablo's words came back to her from when he had first shown her Juan's Gila monster, Diablo. *You have to get down, look into their eyes, then quickly flip them. They don't move fast at all. They are really slow. But if they look in your eyes they sort of freeze, then you flip them.*

But it was Juan's voice that Pablo was hearing now. He could have been a million miles from Georgia.

Do it boy. Juan's words seeped into his head. *You can do it. You breathe steady, you try and match your breath to the beast's. He's picking up your scent. Listen to his breath—the huff huss. You can do that.* Juan's words coursed through his mind. It was as if he were right there whispering in his ear. But he had never dared to do it.

The blue forked tongue darted out now. But the lizard did not move. Slowly Pablo's hand crept toward the creature. Was it his own heartbeat that he was hearing, or the Gila monster's? His own beat was slowing, as if his heart was trying to match the rhythm of the Gila monster. A peace stole through him. The lizard's own eyelids were closing, like when Juan would reach in to grab Diablo. Pablo gazed at his own hand, but in his mind he imagined Juan's hand, old, the knuckles swollen with arthritis, the bulging purple veins, yet very steady, not a tremble.

The movement was sudden but graceful. Pablo's hand had grabbed the lizard behind its front legs and in a split second had flipped the creature over. His fingers began stroking its belly. Its eyelids started to close. The reptile went limp in his hands. "I did it!" His eyes glittered in triumph. He carefully set the lizard aside, still on its back, and scrambled through the hole.

"Will he stay that way?"

"Until he gets hungry."

"When's that?"

"Maybe two weeks if he's just eaten. Not a big eater. We fed Diablo every ten days, or so."

Pablo motioned to Georgia to come up and prayed that she could make it on her own this time and would not need him shoving her bony butt up through the hole, the sipapu, into this glorious light, this sacred light, as both she and Pablo now thought of it.

For it was sacred. This was the place, or a kiva like it, where Pablo would come for his coming-of-age ceremony. Where thirty-one logs from all male trees would be gathered;

where four layers of blankets would be laid down, where forty-eight rocks would be gathered. It was sacred and yet Pablo instantly knew it had been desecrated, the enemy, and was sacred no longer. Pablo could feel it. It had been invaded by white people.

Georgia made it into the kiva and tipped her face toward the stream of sunlight. She basked in it. She could see clouds and birds drifting by. Just beneath the gap, on one ledge there were beautiful pieces of once-whole pots but they were now fractured. All of them bore the rainbow emblem. There was also an altar with early spirit gods that over the course of thousands of years would evolve into the popular Kachina dolls of the Hopi Indians. There were bone tools and petrified wood that rested on an altar-like projection from the wall. Georgia walked over to it and then tipped her head toward the wide opening above to bask some more in the light that poured through. She felt blessed.

She recalled how Stieglitz had once told a magazine reporter, when asked about light: "Light is better than religion. It allows you to see rather than tells you what to do; and therefore, is a reality so subtle that it becomes more real than reality."

This was more than reality. "Oh Stieglitz," she sighed. She sank to the bench below the ledge and looked at Pablo, who was now peering down at the Gila monster with a beatific look on his face.

"Yes, yes . . . don't wake the baby," she whispered,

"There's another canteen of water over there. Someone must have left it." Pablo nodded toward a canteen on the bench.

"Someone? I wonder who," she asked. And then the answer came to her. Orville's words echoed in the back of her mind from the evening they had visited the archaeologists to celebrate the find of the potsherds with the rainbow. "But if this is a sacred site, then the Navajo heritage group is going to raise hell. You know how they are about keeping sacred places sacred. They're trying right now to get laws passed to avoid contamination of sacred places."

Douglas Acheson had been stealing artifacts from a forbidden site. This was a sacred place.

"You know, Miss Georgia, I have a feeling that we shouldn't be here." She turned slowly toward him.

"Yes, so do I, Pablo."

"I think this place is baa hą́ą́h hasin. It's sacred. This is where the shamans come. We don't belong here."

"But we're here now," she replied. "And yes, you're right, we shouldn't be here." She paused. "But you know who has been here?"

"Who's that?" Pablo asked.

"The digging men."

"The digging men . . . you mean the ones who come into the trading post for supplies?"

"Yes, those men."

"But why?"

"They want all this." She gestured to the spirit dolls and the beautiful pots.

"But these are baa hą́ą́h hasin; they are sacred too. They should not be touched by others, and some of them should only be held by shamans during special ceremonies."

"I know this, and they know it too!"

"But they do it anyway?"

"Yes, they do."

"But why?"

"Money, I suppose."

"You mean they sell these things?"

"In a sense, yes, they do. They tell people who give them money for the digging to give them more as they say it is valuable for education, for understanding the ancient people, the Anasazi people."

"But that's wrong!" Pablo hissed. "It's only valuable for us, for Navajo people—for our sand paintings, for our celebration of the corn days, for Hózhóójí. We need them for those ceremonies. They are not for white people."

"What is Hózhóójí?" Georgia asked.

"I can't explain it, but it's good. Everything good—peace—you know . . ." Pablo made his hand flat and then seemed to move his hand ever so slightly in the air. "To be . . . you know . . ."

"Balanced?"

"Yes! To be in balance and at peace . . . peacefulness." Pablo sighed. "This is bad that white people came in here and took these things. Touched these sacred things. They are diyin for the Diné, the Holy People, us. Holy, only a shaman can touch many of these things."

"I'm sorry, Pablo. I am so sorry."

Pablo was still looking down at the Gila monster, who seemed to be in some sort of deep stupor.

"Do you have any idea where we are or what time it is?" Georgia asked.

Pablo turned his head to where the ladder had stood.

Getting up slowly, so as not to disturb the lizard, he turned to Georgia and spoke in a whisper. "I'll get the ladder and look."

"Are you sure it won't wake up?" she asked, nodding at the lizard.

"No, unless I turn him over."

"Please don't."

Pablo tiptoed away, fetched the canteen for Georgia, then brought the ladder back up through the sipapu. He carefully placed it beneath the opening in the ceiling of the kiva that led to the outdoors, which would allow visitors from the cliffs to enter.

Georgia watched him set it up beneath that opening. Then she glanced over at the reptile which could have been dead for all she knew, as there was no sign of its breathing.

"Getting darker," Pablo said.

"How can you tell?"

"All kivas face southeast. Getting close to dinner time."

Suddenly Georgia's stomach growled softly. "Shut up," she whispered. "Don't want to wake the baby." She glanced at Diablo. She surprised herself. She thought of the lizard as Diablo. He looked the same.

Oh God, she thought. I'm really going crazy. What am I doing here? How did I get here? "And where is Juan?" She hadn't realized she had spoken those last four words out loud. But she had.

"Juan is very near, Miss Georgia. He's . . . he's here."

"Did you hear me, Pablo?"

"Yes."

"I didn't realize I was speaking out loud."

"You do sometimes."

"Oh, dear what else have I blabbed about?"

"Oh, I don't know . . . someone named Ryan."

"You don't say?"

"Yep."

"Anyone else?"

"Someone named Rippy."

"Rippy!" she exclaimed.

"Who's Rippy?"

"My sister-in-law's obnoxious, yappy little terrier, not worth a damn." She sighed.

"A terrier? What kind of dog is that?"

"An annoying kind of dog," she replied and Pablo laughed.

"What are you laughing at, Pablo?"

"You."

"Me?"

"Yes."

"Why?"

"You can get very grouchy very fast."

"Give me an example?"

"I just did. The terrier dog."

"Well, the terrier is annoying because its owner is extremely annoying—Alfred's sister, Selma."

"Who's Alfred?"

"My husband."

"Oh . . ." He paused. "Well, who's Ryan then?"

"Whoever mentioned Ryan?" she snapped.

"You did in your sleep. All the time. You talk a lot in your sleep."

"I do?"

"Yes, and someone named Dorothy."

"Oh for God's sake, Dorothy Norman."

"Yes, that's the one. Is she a dog too?"

"No, but she's annoying. Why do you ask?"

"Because you called her a bitch like the other dog, the terrier Rippy."

"Oh, Jesus, I better shut up." Georgia sighed. "No, Dorothy is not a dog, and let's leave it at that."

They were both silent for a while.

"So, Pablo, how long do you think we've been gone?"

"I don't know. Two days maybe? But now we should be able to get out and find our way back."

"Somehow, maybe." Georgia sighed.

"What do you mean 'maybe'?"

"I'm pretty weak, Pablo. But you should go on if I can't make it."

He looked at her, shocked, then walked over and crouched beside her, taking both her hands.

"Don't speak that way, Miss Georgia. I am not leaving you here. I am not going without you."

"As I said, I'm weak. I don't think I can make it to wherever we're going."

"You are not weak." It was not simply a statement; it was a command. Pablo dug into his pocket and took out a Tootsie Roll.

"I thought you said the last one was the one we split?"

"I lied. Now eat this one. And then I'll tell you a story."

"What story?"

"The story of Changing Woman."

Georgia opened her eyes wider. "I like Changing Woman stories. For years now I have painted the Pedernal, a mesa over by the Ghost Ranch. They say it is where Changing Woman was born. Yes, Changing Woman, the daughter of Earth and Sky, I can see the mesa from my casita. I have painted it so many times."

Pablo began to speak. "So, you know the story, how Changing Woman gave birth to the children of the Sun, Johonaa'éí? He shined his rays on her and that's how she got the babies."

"Just a little sunshine and she got babies. How nice," Georgia said.

"You never had babies?"

"No, unfortunately, I never did." She paused. "Not even when I went sunbathing." She laughed.

"Sunbathing, what are you talking about? What is sunbathing? Don't white people bathe in water?"

"Of course they do. To get clean, not to have babies." She laughed.

"Then why do they bathe in the sun?"

"To get a tan."

"Get a tan?"

"Brown color?"

"Their skin?"

"Yes."

"Brown like us?" Pablo asked.

"Well, yes."

"But they don't really like us."

"Some of them do."

"This is very confusing, Miss Georgia."

"It is, Pablo."

He sighed. "So, you never had babies." Conversations with Pablo tended to jump around.

"That's right, never."

"That's too bad. You would have made a good mother."

"You really think so, Pablo?"

"I know so."

Georgia sighed. "Go on with the story, please."

"Changing Woman's children are the twin heroes, Monster Slayer and Child of Water, who cleared the earth of the monsters that once were here."

"And what are their names in Navajo?" Georgia asked. "I forgot."

"Monster Slayer is called Naayéé' neizgháni and Child of Water is named Bajish chini."

"That's right," Georgia murmured and nodded her head. "I remember now."

Pablo smiled. He detected a new energy coursing through her.

"You know, Miss Georgia—"

"You can drop the 'Miss', Pablo. I don't call you Señor Pablo."

He giggled. "You know, Georgia, my cousin and I once

dressed up as Monster Slayer and Child of Water, for the Green Corn Festival."

"That must have been fun."

"Yeah," he sighed. In his eyes Georgia saw a yearning for something. Some past happiness perhaps.

"Anyhow, Changing Woman lives by herself in a house floating on the western waters, where the Sun visits her every evening. One day she became lonely and decided to make some companions for herself. From pieces of her own skin, she created men and women who became the ancestors of our people. Changing Woman also made us corn . . . in the story you see, Changing Woman never dies but she keeps changing all the time. She grows into an old woman in the wintertime and by spring she becomes young again."

"That's nice," Georgia murmured. She closed her eyes as Pablo's voice, almost like a hymn, wove through the dwindling light of the kiva. She saw the paintings she had done of the mesa over the years, the oblique silhouette that had first captivated her. She had painted it in all kinds of light. There was something noble about its profile. *How silly of me.* She thought back to the first time she had painted it. *I thought I could own that mesa. But it's the reverse; Changing Woman owns me . . .*

THIRTY-SIX

Sam Wolfe walked into the President of Yale's office. Charles Dodd rose from his chair and came around his desk to shake Wolfe's hand.

"My secretary said it was urgent."

"Yes, it is," Sam said.

"It's been quite a morning already. So, I doubt if I could get any more upset."

Dodd's usually placid demeanor indeed looked troubled, his eyes slightly watery as if he might have even been crying and there seemed to be a tic of some sort near his left eye that caused him to blink rapidly.

"Well, sir, I have serious doubts about that archaeological dig out in New Mexico."

The president blanched and swayed a bit.

"Are you all right, sir?"

"Forgive me. I need to sit down." Shakily he went back to his desk, took his seat, and availed himself of a glass of water. "You have doubts, you say?"

"Yes, sir, I have it on very good authority that the artifacts that have been excavated might be . . ." He paused and inhaled sharply. "Of dubious provenance. And worse, might have been extracted from sacred land of the Navajo . . ."

President Dodd put his hand to his heart. His shoulders sank. He was still for several seconds before he looked up at Sam.

"Sam, my friend, I have even worse news."

"Worse?"

"Regina Phelps has been murdered."

"B–b–but . . . but I talked to her two days ago and she was the one who aroused my suspicion about the provenance."

"Indeed, and apparently this could be considered a motive for her murder. Although the police are also searching for her stepdaughter, Marya Phelps Armstrong, as she was seen arguing vehemently with Regina. Apparently, it was about the inheritance the late Mr. Phelps left behind to Regina—and Regina only."

"But how can this possibly . . ." Sam's voice trailed off.

"Greed," Dodd answered simply. He looked out the window toward the Regina and Edward Phelps Center for Archaeology and Anthropology building, which had been completed just a year ago.

Dodd sighed. "We'll have to change the name, I think. Hard to defend something like that in the middle of this depression."

Sam rubbed his chin. *Maybe*, he thought, *it is all an indulgence in these times. We obsess over our silly relics of past ages while children are starving during this depression.* Sam's sister worked for an orphanage in Indiana. She drove around southern Indiana picking up children who had been abandoned by their families. Children who were starving. And here he was sitting in the comfy splendor of the Ivy League. Yale with its silly clubs, its worship of patrician patriarchs. No women allowed. A quota on Jews, of course. God forbid a Black man should cross the campus. He got up to leave.

"I can see that the news has shaken you, Sam, as it has myself."

"Yes, yes, I am shaken, sir. As a matter of fact, I might ask for a leave of absence."

"A sabbatical?"

He gave a harsh laugh. "It would be indulgent for me to call it that. Hardly a sabbatical."

"What then?"

The idea popped into his head. Why not? "A leave of absence to help at the orphanage where my sister works in southern Indiana."

"Have you gone mad, young man?"

"Not at all, sir. Not at all."

"But we need you here. Your lab is invaluable in seeking out the stories of the past."

"Yes, stories, that's all." *Stories*, he thought, *of dead people from centuries ago. We stole this land from indigenous peoples and now claim to revere it. Revere and build monuments to it. How much was the new Phelps building said to cost? Almost a million dollars? How does one justify that?*

Sam shakily left the president's office.

"OK, I finished the Tootsie Roll," Georgia said. "Now you can tell me another story. I found that one of Changing Woman quite . . . quite refreshing."

"Let me think for a minute," Pablo said.

"Don't take too long."

"Georgia, you're awfully bossy."

"Oh really," she said with a glint in her eye.

"All right. So, when we were down below, and you were leaning against the rock wall. You reminded me of a spider. Like Spider Woman in the stories my grandmother told me."

"Is that good or bad?"

"Good."

"Why did I remind you of her—a spider?"

"Well, I'm not sure. You know you're awfully skinny and your knees were poking up and your elbows sticking out."

"That accounts for only four limbs. Spiders have eight."

"I know, I know," Pablo said impatiently. "I just said you reminded me of a spider. I didn't say you *were* a spider."

"All right. Go ahead."

"You should be pleased. Spiders are good in the legends. They weave truth with their silk. They straighten out the world. They are the opposite of Coyote who is the trickster and messes everything up."

"Yes." Georgia nodded. "Coyote made the stars a mess when he shook out the star blanket."

"Exactly, and Spider Woman fixed the mess. She knew how to untangle the stars because she was a weaver; she's Na'ashjé'ii Asdzáá."

"Who?"

"Na'ashjé'ii Asdzáá, that's Spider Woman's name in Navajo. She wove the stars into the night so we could find them, keep track of them. She wove them into a web that pointed the ways so we would always know the true direction and never get lost."

"But I paint. I don't weave."

"Does it matter?" Pablo paused a second. "Can I ask you something?"

"Sure, go ahead."

"Why do you paint?"

"I don't know. Maybe like when I paint a flower, I paint it big, bigger than it will ever grow. I suppose it's because I want people to stop and look at it and really catch their breath. I've always believed that colors and shapes can make more of a point than words. So, I guess I paint because I want people to stop and look, really see what's there before them."

"See, you're like Spider Woman the weaver. She weaves to show a person the way."

"But I'm not showing anybody the way to anything."

"You make them pay attention to something. That's showing them."

"Maybe."

"Don't argue with me. You do."

"If you say so," Georgia replied wearily. "So, tell me a good Spider Woman story."

"Well, I'll tell you one my grandmother told me."

"All right."

"You know my grandmother, she was just like Spider Woman. She would always rub her hands in the spiderwebs to help her see the story she was weaving. So do that!"

"Me?"

"Yes you. And I will too."

They both pretended to rub their hands in a non-existent spider web.

"It will still work," Pablo said. "If you believe."

"I believe." Georgia nodded.

"So," Pablo continued. "When people were first created, Spider Woman told them to leave and plant trees to climb into the fourth world. But none of the trees grew tall enough. Then she told them to sing to a bamboo plant so that it would grow very, very tall." Pablo stretched his hands up high and then stood on his tiptoes. "Like we must do here or have done so we can leave the underworld. You see, Georgia, we are still in the Third World."

Georgia nodded. "So we are."

"And it was through the hollow reed of the bamboo stalk that they climbed out to that Fourth World . . . and we shall too. Tomorrow when it is light, and we can see where we are going."

"She grew a tree but did not weave a web for them to climb?" Georgia asked.

Pablo's eyelids were growing heavy.

"Maybe, maybe it was a web, but I forget." He yawned and leaned against the wall of the kiva. And within seconds he was sound asleep. Georgia put a hand lightly to her mouth. She was in awe. How beautiful this young boy looked. How fragile and yet how strong.

The last thing she remembered was that the Gila monster began to stir just as a slice of moonlight pierced through the opening at the top of the ladder. "Baby, go to sleep," she muttered in a thick voice and curled up on the floor.

Tomorrow they would climb out and make their way down the cliffs. Tomorrow she would see Ryan again.

Outside the wind was picking up and soon it was screeching across the night. But Georgia for some reason felt safe. Yes, a possibly deadly monster mere feet away was beginning to awaken, and outside the fierce winds carved the landscape into new configurations. But she was too tired to worry. Was she dying? Is this what it felt like, as death neared? At least this would be a peaceful death—not in battle, not in agonizing pain, just wrapped in ancient rock with winds scraping and sculpting the world into new configurations.

THIRTY-SEVEN

Sam Wolfe had experienced a range of emotions in the past days. First it was the shock of Mrs. Phelps' phone call about her suspicions at the dig, then the horrific news that she had died, and that it was suspected murder. Then grief and fury had set in. He had always thought that Douglas Acheson was a pompous ass. He wore his knowledge like a thin coat of shellac. All shiny but no nuance. There was none of the kind of hypothetical conjecture that roiled in most scholars' brains and that allowed them to contemplate alternative scenarios, or question or doubt. Sam earnestly believed that serious scholars often doubted. Doubt could be a path to truth. Francis Bacon had said: "If we begin with certainties, we shall end in doubts; but if we begin with doubts, and are patient in them, we shall end in certainties." Why or when did doubt get such a bad name? Doubt in Sam's mind was the engine for discovery.

It was ironic then that with little doubt in his mind, he changed course abruptly. He did not go to Indiana to visit his sister and help her pick up abandoned children. There was another objective here, another truth to be revealed that now was more important in his mind.

So, he breezed through Indiana to Chicago where he boarded the railroad, the Atchison, Pacific to Santa Fe. On arriving in Santa Fe, he rented a car and hightailed it to the Bisti Badlands. He had brought with him detailed maps of the dig. He knew that the students had already returned east and that officially the site had been closed. But normally Acheson lingered on for a few days to secure the site. Then he often went on to California to visit a relative. Classes at Yale would not be starting for weeks.

As Sam drove up to the trading post in Far Cry, he stopped

to see if he could get some food, and of course water. It was blistering hot.

"Anybody home?" he shouted, for the store seemed empty.

"Coming," a voice called from a back room.

There was the sound of a crate being moved.

A beautiful young woman came out holding a large box in her arms.

"Here, I can help you with that," he offered.

"OK, there by the freezer, please." They both carried the box over and set it down.

"I have to get this stuff in there fast before it melts."

"Sure, I'll help you," he said.

"Just hold the lid open for me, please."

"Sure thing."

Wynnie turned to Sam when they had finished putting the last carton of popsicles into the deep freeze.

"OK, thanks so much. Want a popsicle, on the house?" She held up the icy treat. "I'll be sold out by noon."

"Yes, if you insist."

"Now, what can I do for you?"

"Well, I'm here from New Haven, Connecticut—Yale University—and I'm—"

"You're here about the archaeology site," she interrupted him.

"Yes . . . uh . . . how did you figure that out so fast?"

"Not hard. How many visitors do you think we get from Yale every year?"

"Not many, I guess."

"Better eat it fast." Wynnie nodded at the grape popsicle he was holding. "They don't last long out here."

"The visitors or the popsicles?" Sam laughed. "So, you're familiar with the site, Miss . . .?"

"Just call me Wynnie. Yes. I helped out there."

"Did you like it?"

She shrugged her shoulders indifferently. "It was OK." He recalled his phone conversation with Regina Phelps and realized that this must be the girl Regina had mentioned, who had expressed discomfort about finding the artifacts.

"Just OK?" He looked at her. Her face had become an impenetrable mask. There was not a flicker of a reaction.

"You helped out."

She barely nodded.

"What did you mostly do?"

Her eyes shifted so she was looking into the shadows of the store. "Mostly worked the screens, sifting for small bits, you know."

"Like potsherds, and that?"

"Yeah, like that."

He realized that he wasn't going to get much more from her.

"Could you direct me to the site?"

"They closed it down, you know."

"Yes, I know. But I still need to see it." He paused. "Take some pictures. Standard documentation."

She merely shrugged, then leaned so she could see around him. "That your car out there?"

"Yes, it is."

"I guess you'll make it. You'll need to go by the Old Sand road. It's right out of town when you're heading south."

"All right, and then what?"

"Here, I'll draw you a map."

There were three regions within close proximity where active excavations had occurred for the past two years. Two of the three had been "put to bed", as they say, with backfill. They could of course be reopened in the coming years. The third was still open, and still exposed, but somewhat protected by light fencing and signs informing anyone visiting—which was unlikely—to kindly stay outside the fencing as this was an active site.

Sam stooped down. He took a pinch of soil and rubbed it between his fingers. It seemed consistent with the soil samples that had already been submitted to his lab with the artifacts from the previous summers. He sighed. *If only.* He thought. *If only there was some absolute way to date the artifacts and test the rocks, the soil, to determine time; to determine absolute chronometric time.* Willard Libby at the University of Chicago was on to something but when he would get there was anybody's guess. It was a technique based on the decay of the carbon-14 isotope. A lot of people had been disdainful. Willard was being held in contempt for butting into a discipline he was not trained in; trying to "cross breed" historical development with science; an "unlikely marriage" between physics and cultural history, surely to produce a bastard in some people's eyes. Now he recalled how Acheson had spoken out vehemently about what he called the "inanity" of absolute chronometric time and the "futility" of tinkering around with the carbon-14 isotope.

Sam stood up, brushed the dirt from his hands, and took in the distant view with his binoculars. A hawk rose directly above him. "Rusty" hawks, they were sometimes called, because of their reddish plumage. This was one of the most striking landscapes he had ever seen in the west. He followed the hawk as it flew over the multicolored moonscape below with its expanse of black hills. This was where the dinosaurs died, and the age of mammals began. There were hoodoos, the spire rock formations, as well as the mushroom-shaped ones. All sculpted by wind and erosion into myriad odd shapes. At first glance it appeared to be a limited palette of rock, mostly gray. But if one looked harder, there was ample evidence of four different rock sequences. There were gray shales, along with white sandstone, concretions of iron minerals and colors that varied from brown to purple and even green rocks. A geologist could spend a lifetime here.

Sam's eyes drifted over to the western cliffs. It was red rock shale for the most part—"clinker" rock as it was often called, or "red dog", as it provided the brightest color in the generally subdued Bisti Badlands' palette. He adjusted his binoculars and focused on the cliffs. Some sort of tree grew there. Always such a surprise seeing a living tree spring from rock—from shale, coal, and sandstone. But juniper, pinyon and bristlecone pine seemed to thrive. They possessed remarkable survival strategies and flourished where others could not. Perhaps like the people of this land, spreading their roots as far as possible, clinging to steep cliffs, they survived. But what was it that cut down Regina Phelps? How could this have happened? The sky was darkening ominously now. It appeared as if some weather might be coming in. He'd better be on his way. The woman at the trading post had directed him to a motel in Shiprock where he might be able to stay.

THIRTY-EIGHT

"My God, it's like a maze here, a maze of hoodoos," Ryan McCaffrey exclaimed. It was as if the tall skinny shafts of rock sculpted by wind and weather had now melted together. "From a distance this looked like just cliffs, but look at them all bunched up here." The sheriff and his deputy, Joe Descheeni, had taken refuge beneath a rock overhang as the haboob, the wind, erupted near dawn and was blowing sand around them. They covered their faces with their hats and pulled up their shirts as high as they could. There were stories of people who had died of sand impaction out in this country when haboobs blew. "Severe hypoxemia." The first time Ryan had heard those words was when he was about six or seven years old. The two words had popped out of the coroner's mouth as he stood over the body of a next-door neighbor's young child who had been snatched up along with his infant sister. He could recall the coroner standing there, holding the infant upside down by its tiny feet and slapping it on the back as sand poured from its mouth. The worst haboob on record. That could have been the moment that Ryan stopped believing in God. Why would God pick those two children who lived next door to Ryan and not him? Why them? The image of that baby hanging upside down by its heels from the coroner's hand was seared into his brain.

"I think it's stopping," Joe said.

"That's what you said fifteen minutes ago," Ryan replied.

"My hat's not working to keep the sand out. I'm going to try stripping down to my undershirt and tie my shirt over my face."

"Try your undershirt instead. It will work better to filter out the sand—light material."

"Good point."

Both men struggled with their shirts.

Ryan had just peeled off his undershirt and tied it around his mouth when a blast of wind came through and snatched the shirt he had been wearing from where he had dropped it on the ground.

"Ah shit!" Ryan cursed. "Look, the wind stole my shirt!" He watched through the gale of sand as the shirt took wing.

It flapped overhead like a peculiar plaid bird.

"Lucky you didn't take off your pants." Joe laughed.

Ryan's heart skipped a beat as he remembered Georgia on the last morning they had seen other. *How about one for the road before you go?* She had walked right over to him and pulled down his pants. Goddam that woman was sassy. What would he do without her?

Finally, the wind died down. They sat and began to pour sand and grit out of their boots and shake it from their hair and clothes. The tall spires of tent rocks—fairy chimneys—stippled the scenery. It was easy to become disoriented in this landscape as Ryan and his deputy were soon discovering. Although they had thought that Douglas Acheson and Gideon Blake were less than a quarter of a mile ahead of them, they had lost them when the haboob struck.

"Obviously we took the wrong turn back there, just before the haboob," Joe said, passing his canteen to Ryan. "I mean, I thought we were on their trail. But now I'm not sure. It's like everything has been rearranged."

Ryan sighed. Navajos were known for their tracking skills, but not him. His late wife Mattie used to joke that he couldn't find his way through a grocery store, but his deputy came from a long line of Navajo trackers that were often employed by the state and federal government. These trackers eventually became known as Shadow Wolves. They could find not simply footprints or tire tracks, but myriad traces of physical evidence left by humans. They could even discern from a footprint how heavy the person was, and if that person was stopping, or turning, or shifting weight.

"Maybe they were just blown away. I wonder how this impacted the search in the sinkhole. God, I hope it didn't fill up again after all that excavation," Ryan muttered.

"Think of it another way, Sheriff. Maybe they were safe during that haboob."

"Safe? How so?" He took a deep breath. "Tell me honestly, Joe. What do you think the chances are of finding Georgia and that boy alive?"

Joe didn't know what to say. Truthfully, he didn't think there was a chance, but one never knew. Sinkholes were curious phenomena. He recalled from his childhood that an entire building in Utah was swallowed by a sinkhole. It happened to be a bank. So, people idiotically thought they would find money and began exploring around only to trigger another sinkhole that killed twenty more people. But then he remembered that some sinkholes have vertical walls made of karst and Permian limestone. If Georgia and the young boy had discovered a crack, it might be a way out. He looked up at the cliffs above on the trail.

"Those cliffs are limestone. Lots of caves and caverns." Joe pointed toward the same cliffs.

"And if I might ask, what does that have to do with the price of eggs?"

"Well, there could be cracks leading to caverns and such. If in fact one such crack was revealed and Georgia or the boy spotted it, they might be able to get to it and maybe they could survive." He paused. "Maybe."

"And might I remind you that the sinkhole occurred almost half a mile or more from those cliffs—below those cliffs." He paused. "And no offense intended but, Deputy Descheeni, since when did you become a geologist?"

"I never became one. I just took a few courses in geology in college. So maybe if they could find refuge in a cave or something they could survive."

"Maybe," Ryan said. The word "maybe" was like a tattered prayer in his mind. He sighed. "We better keep going."

It was almost more restful to think about crooked archaeologists than Georgia and the boy in that sinkhole. But, of course, first they had to find these archaeologists, or the sacred site they had been pilfering from.

They had been walking for about twenty minutes from their

last rest stop when Joe, who was in the lead, turned to his boss and raised a hand to stop him, then put a finger to his lips signaling to be quiet.

They both froze in their footsteps. Ahead they heard voices. Quite clearly.

"I got the backfill for strata six. I figure we got enough to potentially get us through the next two seasons."

"And hopefully another benefactor."

How many angels can dance on the head of a pin when one angel has been murdered? Ryan wondered.

THIRTY-NINE

The wind had died down. Pablo had woken up. He looked across at Georgia. It seemed to him that she had shrunk. She looked like a dried corn husk. Dried and shriveled. He knew where they were now, up in the cliffs. To get down would be treacherous, for the terrain was steep. He noticed something odd where the ladder normally stood beneath the entrance to the kiva. Something was blocking the hole. It was preventing the sunlight from shining down. And if there was one thing he and Georgia craved, it was sunlight. He glanced at the Gila monster, still in a stupor on its back. The last thing he wanted to do was wake it up. He moved the ladder quietly and propped it beneath the opening. Then, climbing up, he reached for what appeared to be a cloth of some sort that had been blocking the light.

"Whatcha got there?" Georgia asked, propping herself up on her elbow.

"Not sure. Piece of clothing or something."

Georgia squinted. It took several seconds for the pattern to emerge and when it did it was as if a current had jolted her brain. "That's plaid! Plaid, Pablo!" she exclaimed as if it was the most marvelous thing in the world. And it was not just any plaid. It was Ryan's shirt. Impossible! "Bring that here, Pablo. Bring that here immediately."

He scrambled down the ladder. Georgia grabbed the shirt from him. "Oh my God!" she squealed. She pressed the shirt against her face. "How did it get here? And in one piece." She shook it out. "One piece except for the rip that I told him to mend."

"What . . . what are you talking about, Georgia?"

She reached out and grabbed Pablo. Her face was wet with tears. "He must be near . . . he must be near and half naked." Pablo had no idea what she was babbling about. Plaid?

Something about telling him to mend it? It all seemed like gibberish to Pablo.

Suddenly there was the sound of footsteps. "Ryan! Ryan!" she called out. She sprang from where she had been sleeping and began scrambling up the ladder with more energy than Pablo had thought was in her. She poked her head through the hole only to be greeted by an unexpected but familiar face. A face with a very grim expression.

"We've got a problem here, Professor."

"What is it?" said another familiar voice. "Oh my goodness. This is not good."

Why am I not good? Georgia wondered, but only briefly. Pablo was right behind her, hidden away.

"What are you doing here?" Georgia said hoarsely.

"Get the fuck off this ladder!" the younger man growled. His mouth twisted into an ugly snarl. She heard Pablo gasp, then she fell back, and they both tumbled to the floor of the kiva.

How long had it been since Pablo had heard a voice other than Georgia's? His first instinct was to yell for help. But he instantly realized that it was risky. They were somewhere they were not supposed to be—a sacred site. Even though they were not stealing artifacts from the site, they had violated a sacred place just by being there. In that sense they were no better than the archaeologists who had been stealing artifacts. Pablo shut his eyes. If these white people, the diggers, were really bad, he did not want to think about what they might do to him and Georgia. Then again, shamans could be fierce if their places were violated. And this most definitely had been one of their places. It was close to where the dead were taken on boards, to be placed high in the juniper trees, where no chindi would follow.

Sprawled on the floor of the kiva, Georgia and Pablo exchanged desperate glances. Pablo was cradling the Gila monster in his arms—it seemed to still be in its hypnotic state. But all three of them were trapped. Where could they go? Back down through the sipapu to wind endlessly through that infinity of tunnels? Georgia glanced at the Gila monster, capable of killing them both, and then at the pair of boots descending the ladder. She sighed. Truly the definition of being between a rock and a hard place.

Pablo, with the still-sleeping reptile in his arms, moved toward the sipapu just as the archaeologist's foot set down on the last rung of the ladder.

"So, what have we here?" Gideon Blake said. Both Georgia and Pablo froze where they stood. The foot of the second man appeared above. The ladder creaked just a bit. Then Blake turned around as he stepped off the ladder. He squinted as he caught sight of Georgia leaning against the wall.

"Do my eyes deceive me? But I believe we have company. Look at our welcome committee, Professor Acheson," he said hoarsely.

"My goodness," Acheson said. "Yes, company. Distinguished company at that! Thought you vanished in a sinkhole, Miss O'Keeffe."

"No," Georgia whispered hoarsely.

"This is not where you're supposed to be."

"Nor you, Professor," she replied.

They did not seem to see Pablo, who was pressed in the shadows near the sipapu. Georgia rose from her position on the floor. Slowly, almost languidly. The thrum of her heart was so loud it was as if it filled the space.

"Can you believe this?" Blake's eyes slid toward the professor. "What's she doing here?"

"We might ask," Acheson said.

"No!" Georgia barked. "What are *you* doing here?"

At that moment Pablo rushed from the shadows and flung the Gila monster at Blake's chest.

"Jesus Christ!" he screamed. Blood spurted from his neck as the reptile buried his teeth into the skin.

Acheson stood paralyzed as he watched blood spurt all over Blake. Georgia could not tear her eyes away from this spectacle. She saw Blake attempt to raise his arms, but they ricocheted spasmodically in the air. The Gila monster clamped down harder on him.

"Get it off!" Acheson screamed. "Get it off!" His face was distorted with rage.

Blake's arms went limp. Then his chest heaved as he fell to the ground.

Acheson's face turned ashen. "You killed him! You bitch!" he exclaimed as he lunged at Georgia.

Pablo suddenly seemed to become airborne. He leaped across the earthen floor onto Acheson's back and began tearing at his hair.

"Did you hear that?" Outside, Ryan McCaffrey turned to his deputy.

"Yes," He took a deep breath. "Someone screamed."

The trail had flattened and both men began to run. Less than a minute later they saw a ladder emerging through some brush.

"A kiva ladder!" Joe said.

The sight that met them as they climbed down the kiva ladder was unbelievable. One man was on the floor of the kiva with a Gila monster lapping up the blood that flowed from his neck with its forked tongue.

The creature turned to regard the two men coming down the ladder and disengaged from the neck of Gideon Blake, then ambled away languorously as if it had all the time in the world.

Another man was crumpled nearby in a state of shock. Then a child's voice came out of the shadows. "Don't worry, he won't bite. And they are very slow when they move."

"And who are you?" Ryan asked.

Pablo walked out of the shadows.

"My name is Pablo Jemez. My mother is from the Bear People clan and my father from the Bitter Water clan, but they died a long time ago, and this is my friend Miss Georgia O'Keeffe." He turned toward Georgia who was slumped against the wall, still clutching Ryan's plaid shirt.

"Georgia!" Ryan gasped. "How the hell did you get here?"

"Lost your shirt, didn't you?" She held up the shirt.

"But how did you get here?"

"It's a long story, my dear."

"I have all the time in the world."

Ryan ran to her side and embraced her.

"I'm fine. I'm fine." But then she seemed to simply fade away as if the effort of speaking was too much.

Georgia heard voices and felt herself being lifted on to some sort of board, then a blanket was covering her, and straps tightening around her legs and chest.

Oh my God, she thought, *they're taking me to the junipers . . . of course . . . and this stiff cloth is the canvas that they wrap dead bodies in so the vultures won't tear them apart . . . but I'm not dead, not dead . . . I'm not a body!* She tried to talk, then began to scream, but it was as if something was muffling her voice. She felt the straps tighten . . . *They are going to bury me alive . . . or hang me up in a tree alive . . . This is all a terrible mistake . . . How do I tell them this . . . No one is hearing me . . . no one is listening to me . . .*

She felt a pinch on her arm and then a prick. Where was she? Strapped onto a board of some sort, so tightly she could not wiggle a toe. Trees loomed above her. She still clenched the plaid shirt. The thoughts continued clattering in her head. *My God, am I dead? Is this my funeral? They're taking me to the trees?*

"Am I dead?" Her voice cracked.

"No, Georgia!"

"Ryan?"

"Right here, dear."

She felt another needle stick in her arm.

"Where am I?"

"You're in an ambulance, Georgia," Ryan said softly

"Pablo?"

"Yes."

She opened her eyes wide. Pablo was on one side of her and Ryan was on the other. She heard a police siren in the distance.

"What's going on?"

"I'm right here," Ryan said. "And if you let go of my shirt, I promise to mend it." He leaned down and whispered in her ear. "At least before you pull my pants down."

"What a card you are, Sheriff!" Georgia muttered. "Where's Pablo?"

"Right here, Georgia. I'm holding your hand."

"Oh, Pablo dear, are you all right? You're not dead like me?"

"You're not dead, Georgia," Pablo said.

"Just severely dehydrated," Joe offered.

"You're here too, Joe?"

"Yes, Mam."

"And . . . and . . . where are the . . ."

"Bad guys?" Ryan said.

"Yes, they are really bad . . . really bad."

"We know that, Miss O'Keeffe," Joe said. "Tommy Tso is up there with three Navajo cops from Shiprock. They'll be bringing them down."

"I'd prefer not to see them."

Ryan chuckled. "They aren't going to see anything but the inside of a jail cell for quite a while."

The next day, Georgia was sitting up in a hospital bed in Farmington with a cup of tea and a newspaper. Ryan was sitting next to her. He was also reading the paper.

"Don't worry, Georgia, there's no mention of you. Only the arrest of Professor Douglas Acheson and his sidekick Gideon Blake."

"Thank God there's nothing in the papers. Stieglitz would be having fits." She paused. "But where's Pablo?"

"Right here!" a voice said, and Pablo popped his head around the door. "I brought you more Tootsie Rolls."

"Oh, Pablo, dear! Come give me a hug. Watch out for all the tubes. They have me trussed up like a turkey," she cautioned.

As she hugged him, she thought, *We never did find Juan Nez.*

"But we did," Pablo said.

"We did what?"

"We found Juan, Georgia."

"Did I say that out loud?"

"Yeah, I guessed you were thinking that. You said it a lot in the ambulance and before you woke up here."

"Pablo, what are you talking about? You found Juan?"

"Yes." Pablo smiled.

"How do you figure that?"

"He became Diablo, the Gila monster in the kiva."

"What?"

"Diablo escaped when we were gone. Miss Lucille at the trading post was really scared. But I told her not to be. That we saw him in the cliffs."

"And you knew this."

"Yes, when he let me flip him over so he would go into his sleep. I just knew it in that moment." He paused a bit. "Well, not exactly right then. I knew in the seconds before when I looked in its eyes. I knew that I was truly looking into the eyes of Juan Nez. And the Gila monster looked back at me, and you know what?"

"What?"

"He winked at me, just the way Juan always did."

There was no way that Ryan was going to tell them the truth about Juan Nez right now. He would not destroy their dream. But who knew, was it really just a dream?

FORTY

Three days later, Georgia was back at her casita at the Ghost Ranch. Ryan had bought two copies of the *New Mexican*, billed as the West's oldest newspaper. "Well, I'll be . . ." Georgia said. "Did you read this?"

"What?" asked Ryan.

She began to read out loud from the paper. "San Juan county police officers have found the body of Juan Nez. The body discovered in a recently opened sinkhole in Canyon Ridge, ten miles from Far Cry, New Mexico, was determined to be that of Juan Nez. Mr. Nez had been a resident of Far Cry and had been missing for several weeks, authorities say. Investigators said in a news conference on Wednesday that the cause of death is still unknown, but the body of Mr. Nez appears to have been assaulted by an ax, which severed his left shoulder.

"It says here, Ryan, that it is speculated that Mr. Nez was murdered, and the murder might be linked to another death for which a Professor Douglas Acheson is being held. It is suspected that he and his assistant, the late Gideon Blake of Yale University, was an accomplice in Mr. Nez's murder and that of Mrs. Regina Phelps, who was a major benefactor of a significant archaeological excavation by Yale University." She continued reading the article aloud.

"The excavation in the Canyon Ridge region of the Bisti Badlands sits squarely on top of one of the richest archaeological regions in the United States. Federal law-enforcement agencies are being called in, citing the archaeological and cultural protection act for tribal and sacred lands."

She turned to Ryan. "Oh dear," she whispered. A tear began to roll down her cheek. Ryan reached for her hand. "That dear, dear man." She sighed, remembering that moment when she had first spied the antlers, the ribbon from Juan's braid snagged on one of the tines. "You know, Ryan, I think when

Juan found those antlers—that night—he must have crossed paths with his murderers. They must have left the antlers, killed him, and then dragged his body away to hide it in the brush or some place. And then when the sinkhole caved in, it had disappeared."

"But why would they kill him?" Ryan asked.

"He must have sensed what they were doing. Maybe they had just come down from the cliffs and the kiva and saw him. Wynnie had her suspicions. That was why you and Joe started up the cliffs."

"Indeed, but I was very doubtful of Wynnie's suspicions. I thought this was a dispute about money gone wrong between Mrs. Phelps and her stepdaughter Marya. But they found Marya and questioned her and it turns out she wasn't even near the county when Regina was killed."

"Ah, yes." Georgia nodded. "And what about Regina Phelps? She must have had her suspicions too."

"Oh, definitely. They say she was killed with chloroform which was stolen from a vet clinic just days before her murder."

"Chloroform? What's that about?"

"Oh, maybe you didn't read that article in the paper two days ago when you were still in the hospital."

"Oh dear, I might have been a little ga-ga from all the medicine they gave me."

"Well, that's how they killed Regina Phelps—with lots of chloroform."

The phone rang. Georgia got up to answer it.

"Oh, Alfred!"

"You sound a little tuckered, my dear?"

"No, Alfred. Fit as a fiddle. But it's been extremely hot out here. However, it's already getting cooler."

"So, I was reading about that Yale archaeological scandal out there in the Beast lands—that's what they call it, right? Your Black Place?"

"It's called the Bisti Badlands."

"Did you meet that Yale professor?"

"Very briefly."

"So, when are you coming home?"

"Well, not for a while. As I said, the heat is getting less intense, and fall is such a pretty season out here. I have some catching up to do."

"I'm having to spend a lot of time at Lake George. Doing some renovations, you know. Easier to do it when the family's not there."

This translated in Georgia's mind that it was easier to carry on with Dorothy Norman and go skinny dipping in the lake when the family was not there. But she just nodded and said, "Of course, dear." She looked over at Ryan, who was preparing drinks to take up on the roof. It was almost sunset and the Pedernal, the mesa of Changing Woman, would be at its best. The light was extraordinary. Stieglitz would never understand this part of her life, nor could she understand his inexorable draw to other women. Dorothy Norman was one of the brighter ones. But he did not limit himself. She thought of some of the others—the naked typist. What was her name?

Georgia glanced down at her hand. There was still a purple bruise where the intravenous tube had been inserted to rehydrate her. She would write Pablo. He must have heard about Juan by now. She intended to invite him to come visit. Tommy Tso said he could drive him to the Ghost Ranch. She had promised to show Pablo her globe.

"So," Stieglitz said on the other end. "See you in September?"

"Well, maybe October," Georgia replied.

"I'll miss you, Fluffy," he said, using his occasional nickname for her.

"And I you." It was not a lie. She would but she was not ready for him just yet.

She hung up as Ryan came in and raised a glass, nodding his head.

"Can you make it to the roof for cocktails?"

"Of course I can! But first I want to write a note to Pablo. I promised to write him."

So, she sat down at her desk and took a piece of paper. Print, she reminded herself. Very few people could read her script.

Pablo dearest,

I know you must have heard by now about our dear friend Juan. I know how much he meant to you as your godfather. We both have so many memories of him. And I do believe that the Gila monster we both spent time with carries his spirit.

But on a happier note. When can you come and visit me? Remember I promised to show you the world!

Your friend,

Georgia

EPILOGUE

"OK, dear, I'm right behind you. The drinks are waiting for us up there."

The minute Georgia stepped on the roof of her casita, she knew she was back, really back where she truly belonged. Changing Woman was waiting for her in all her finery. The mesa was gilded in the golden summer light.

"There she is!" Ryan said as he looked out at the view with her.

"You know, dear, I have an idea. I am always painting her at sunset. But . . ."

"But what?"

"Well, I don't know why I never thought of this before, but I think tomorrow I might paint her at dawn."

"But at dawn the mesa is to the west and the sun will be rising in the east."

"That's just the point. She's climbing into the light, out of the darkness. Just like I did." Georgia could feel the shadows gathering behind her. The shadows of the coming night that would soon smother the mesa in darkness. But what would Changing Woman look like in the gray of the dawn? Perhaps like a misty old lady limping through the remnants of darkness but with hope for light.

After all, hope must begin in darkness, she thought.

SEVERN
HOUSE